BOOKS BY FRANK L. COLE

The Afterlife Academy

The World's Greatest Adventure Machine

THE WORLD'S GREATEST ADVENTURE MACHINE

Frank L. Cole

DELACORTE PRESS

Text copyright © 2017 by Frank L. Cole
Jacket art copyright © 2017 by Elizabet Vukovic

All rights reserved. Published in the United States by Delacorte Press, an imprint of Random House Children's Books, a division of Penguin Random House LLC, New York.

Delacorte Press is a registered trademark and the colophon is a trademark of Penguin Random House LLC.

Visit us on the Web! randomhousekids.com

Educators and librarians, for a variety of teaching tools, visit us at RHTeachersLibrarians.com

Library of Congress Cataloging-in-Publication Data is available upon request.

ISBN 978-0-399-55282-3 (hc)
ISBN 978-0-399-55283-0 (ebook)

The text of this book is set in 12-point Minion.
Interior design by Ken Crossland

Printed in the United States of America
10 9 8 7 6 5 4 3 2 1
First Edition

To Marilyn and Frank for never doubting

CHAPTER 1

TREVOR ISAACS SAT in the passenger seat of the faded red Buick, his face pressed against the window. Out on the front lawn of the middle school, Principal Sullinger was bringing Trevor's mom up to speed on Trevor's latest stunt. Ms. Sullinger's expression was grim, and her hands were gesturing wildly.

Trevor's mom alternated between nodding and smiling at Ms. Sullinger, and shooting laser-like glares at Trevor. She was going to kill him. And bury him in the backyard next to Kittles the guinea pig.

After ten grueling minutes, the conversation finally ended, and Trevor's mom walked briskly toward the parking lot. She slid into her seat, slammed the car door shut, and gripped the steering wheel with both hands.

"Why, Trevor, why?" she asked, keeping her voice under control. "I had to leave work again. I can't keep doing that." Trevor's mom was still wearing her scrubs and her name badge. Her hair looked like it had fought valiantly against an electric eggbeater and lost. "We're barely making it as it is. If I lose my job, we'll lose the house."

Trevor stared at the floor of the car and kicked the backpack resting at his feet. "I'm sorry, Mom. I wasn't thinking."

"You've managed to ruin yet another field trip. And now you're banned from the East Chester Museum! Who gets banned from a museum?" She yanked the car into reverse and backed out of the parking lot. "We're just lucky your principal didn't make me pay for the emergency bus transportation. I had to practically beg her for mercy. And I can't *believe* you've been suspended."

"It's not like they'll hold me back or anything," Trevor said, digging at the dirt under his thumbnail. "It's the last week of school, and I'm done with all my testing."

"It's still a suspension." She squeezed the steering wheel, and Trevor could hear the vinyl cover squeaking in protest. "You've gotten into trouble before, but never like this. Your teachers have always understood and have graciously overlooked our situation, but that's not going to happen anymore."

As they approached a stoplight just outside the school grounds, Trevor noticed a couple of his classmates walking along the sidewalk, lugging their backpacks. They turned to see what car was approaching, and a big smile stretched across Hoyt Franklin's face.

"You're crazy!" Hoyt shouted, cupping his hands around his mouth. "Is your mom taking you to jail?"

"Who are those boys?" Trevor's mom asked. "Friends of yours?"

"That's Hoyt Franklin and Eric Palmer." The two boys had stopped walking and now stood on the curb pointing at Trevor and laughing. "They're not really my friends."

"You could've been seriously injured, or worse. And you put your whole school through that," she said. "Did you know Ms. Dobson fainted? Don't you roll your eyes at me!"

"Mom, she always faints. A few weeks ago, a kid got a deep paper cut and Ms. Dobson passed out in her chair. They had to use some awful-smelling powder to wake her up. Besides, no one was even on the lower level where it happened, and it was just a model." He rolled down his window. It was almost summer, and the car's air conditioner had never properly functioned.

Trevor's mom glanced sideways at him. "You're missing the point. Real airplane or not, you crashed it! You almost destroyed an entire World War II display."

"I didn't do it on purpose."

"Oh, so you're saying you accidentally climbed down from the balcony onto the plane?"

"I dropped my phone," Trevor said. "Someone bumped

my arm when we were heading to the next exhibit. What was I supposed to do? Just leave it?"

"You don't think about consequences. I'll be getting a bill for this for sure, and it won't be cheap." She took a deep breath, held it, and then forced the air out through her nostrils. "What's going to happen now? Hmm? What do you think, Trevor?"

He raised his eyebrows and sighed. "I'm going to be grounded."

"You betcha," she said.

"No electronics, no movies, no outside, no nothing." He counted off the list of punishments on his fingers.

Her eyes softened a bit. "You can still play with your friends."

"What friends?" Trevor asked. "I don't have any friends."

"Don't give me that. What about that Jordan Stinks boy? He seems fun."

"It's Stiggs, Mom. Jordan Stiggs," Trevor said. "And his parents grounded him from me for the summer." If Stiggs's parents didn't want him near Jordan, no parent would let their kids hang out with him, especially once word got out about the incident at the museum, and word traveled fast in Decatur, Illinois.

"Maybe that's because you keep putting yourself in extreme danger. And I know you can't help it sometimes—"

"I *can* help it," Trevor interrupted her. "I'm not stupid."

"I've never said you were stupid. No one thinks that. It's just your condition. It's not your fault you have a misfiring amygdala. But it is your responsibility to think things through. Just because you can't feel fear doesn't mean you can't think about consequences."

"Mom, I know. But I wasn't going to get hurt. I landed that plane just fine." No one ever understood. Maybe Trevor saw things differently from other kids, but he hated it whenever his mom talked about his *condition*.

"Great. Now who's that?"

Trevor looked up to see a sleek black car with tinted windows parked in front of their house. A man with wavy blond hair and dark sunglasses stood at the front door. He was casually dressed, in blue jeans and a bright yellow T-shirt. As the Isaacses pulled into the driveway, the man waved, but Trevor's mom did not return the gesture. She parked, checked her makeup in the rearview mirror, and climbed out of the car.

"Hello there. Are you Ms. Isaacs?" The man stepped down from the porch, holding a black briefcase in one hand.

"You must be from the museum? Please, call me Patricia."

"The museum?" The man crinkled his forehead. "No, most definitely not."

"Then where are you from? The school? Is this about Trevor?" She clenched her jaw, awaiting the verdict on Trevor.

The man smiled. "I had one heck of a time trying to find this place. Took the wrong exit. Couldn't seem to reach you on the phone either. I like to call first." He had a sort of laid-back voice that reminded Trevor of a surfer's, only not as thick. Maybe a retired surfer. There was something familiar about it as well, although Trevor couldn't quite put his finger on it. "To answer your question, I'm not from any school, but this does concern your son."

Trevor narrowed his eyes as he noticed the emblem on the man's shirtsleeve. An emblem that looked oddly like a small red castle flanked by two capital letter *C*s. "Oh, no way!" He leapt onto the hood of his mom's car and rolled to the other side, plopping down onto the driveway with a muffled thump.

His mom gasped. "What on earth—"

"I'm fine." Trevor shrugged and brushed the gravel from his elbows before racing up to the porch for a closer look.

The man chuckled. "Well, that was entertaining. You took a bit of spill there, didn't you?"

"It doesn't even hurt," Trevor said. "I know exactly who you are. You're Doug Castleton."

The man nodded. "That's right."

Trevor clamped his hands to the sides of his head. "Mom"—he waved her over—"it's Doug Castleton!"

His mom remained rooted next to her car. "And who exactly is that?"

Trevor's mouth fell open. How could she not know? "Doug Castleton's the owner of CastleCorp. I've watched all their videos. That stratosphere skydive was awesome! What are you doing at my house?" He jabbed the CastleCorp emblem on Doug's arm with his finger.

"Trevor! What has gotten into you?" his mom demanded.

"It's okay, Patricia. The boy is excited, and rightfully so. It's not every day you win a worldwide contest."

Trevor's mom climbed the porch and looked at Trevor suspiciously. "You entered a contest? When?"

"Months ago," Trevor said, rubbing his hands together. "But I didn't think I'd actually win."

"Where are you from, Mr. Castleton?" she asked.

"He comes from Beyond," Trevor answered.

"Oh, good grief. Would you just let the man talk?"

Doug smiled and nodded. "Actually, Trevor's right. I come from Beyond. Beyond, California, that is. Right on the edge of the West Coast, not quite to Oregon, but close enough to the ocean that you can smell the surf." He took a deep, blissful breath. "The most righteous smell of all."

Trevor's mom looked apprehensive, but then the hint of a smile began to form on her lips as she glanced at Doug. "Well, what is it, then?" she asked. "What did he win?"

Doug placed a hand on Trevor's shoulder. "A ride. *The* ride of a lifetime. One that will revolutionize the way we seek thrills on this planet. We're talking the highest drops, the fastest spins and loops, the most breathtaking landscapes." He paused, caught up in his own vision. "Trevor is one of four lucky contestants to win a spot on the maiden voyage of the Adventure Machine." Doug motioned to the Isaacses' front door. "Should we step inside and discuss the details?"

Trevor shook his head in disbelief. It had to be a joke. He never won anything. Not even free fries from Chauncey Burger's Annual Scratch-Off Game. "I won!" he shouted in disbelief, shaking both fists above his head in jubilation. In a matter of minutes, Trevor's day had transformed from a disaster to the best ever.

CHAPTER 2

WISPS OF SMOKE swirled toward the ceiling as the smell of burning pumpernickel bread wafted out of Beatrice Kiffing's oven. Ms. Kiffing was reclining on one of the dining room chairs, sipping an icy beverage.

The smoke detector gave two warning chirps as it inhaled the plumes, and then exploded with a raucous clatter. Ms. Kiffing winced and set her drink down quickly. Just as she jumped out of her chair, the telephone in the kitchen started ringing. She hurried toward the oven, fanning her hand above her head at the smoke detector. Beatrice turned to the phone and was about to answer, when the sound of several screaming teenagers erupted from the hallway.

"Oh, for crying out loud!" Beatrice barked.

Two young girls and a boy appeared in the doorway, coughing from the smoke as Beatrice, now wearing lobster-shaped oven mitts, removed the black loaf of charred bread from the stove.

"It's just a little crispy!" she shouted above the sound of the alarm and the relentlessly ringing telephone. "No need to be so upset. I can scrape most of this off."

One of the girls shook her head. "We're not upset about that, Ms. Kiffing. It's your son."

Beatrice dropped the bread onto the kitchen counter with a thud and then once more went to work, vigorously fanning the smoke detector. "Is Cameron being too hard on you? He can be quite difficult when it comes to tutoring. Just tell him I said to lighten up."

"I'm not going back in there," the boy said. "Not until he puts his clothes back on."

The trilling alarm finally ceased overhead, and the phone gave one final ring before falling silent. In the sudden quiet, Beatrice stared at the three disturbed teens, puffed out her cheeks, and rolled her eyes.

Down the hallway and through the third door on the left, eleven-year-old Cameron Kiffing stood on his bed, rapidly scribbling equations across his window with a dry-erase marker. The small boy mumbled to himself, steadying his glasses on the bridge of his nose, his once-neatly-parted blond hair having morphed into a wild cocoon of dandelion fluff.

"Cameron, honey, you've caused a bit of a fuss with your friends," Ms. Kiffing announced from the entrance of his room. She held the cordless phone at her side, her other hand still swallowed up in the mouth of one of her lobster oven mitts.

"They're my *students,*" Cameron said breathlessly. "And they were the ones who caused the fuss. I merely needed to answer their preposterous question in the simplest way. There!" He spun around, gesturing at a single digit near the bottom of his window. "I told you. Didn't I say—" Cameron blinked, scrunching his nose. "Where did they go?"

"Home. What have I told you about taking your clothes off when we have company over?"

Cameron glanced down at his pinkish, freckled skin, completely naked with the exception of a pair of Star Wars boxers. He scratched an ear and scanned the room, locating his khaki pants, socks, and turtleneck wadded up in a pile by his dresser. "That can't be helped," he said with a shrug. "You know how it is, mother. A brilliant mind shouldn't be constricted."

"But they're loose-fitting. Even the tag says so." His mom fished the pair of pants from the crumpled pile and tossed them to Cameron. Then she jumped as the phone in her hand started to ring again.

"Must be a telemarketer," she said, squinting at the caller ID. "Don't know why anyone from California would be calling me."

"Did you say California?" Cameron zipped up his pants, his head popping out of his turtleneck like a glob of toothpaste from the tube. "What part? Answer it quickly before they hang up!"

"You just worry about your socks, dear. Hello?" Ms. Kiffing asked into the receiver. "Yes, this is his mother."

Cameron silently watched her from his perch atop his mattress, listening intently. Viewed through his thick-lensed glasses, his eyes looked as if they had grown to the size of plums.

"Uh-huh," she said. "He has, has he?" Ms. Kiffing's brow furrowed and she glanced at Cameron suspiciously. "And what exactly has he won?"

Cameron crowed like a rooster and leapt from his bed. Had he been even three or four inches taller, he might have crashed into the ceiling fan.

CHAPTER 3

AT LEAST A hundred spectators were wedged shoulder to shoulder in the tight aisles of the Giggling Gargoyle Arcade, blocking the token machines and the rows of abandoned Skee-Ball lanes. They stood pointing their cell phone cameras toward the Gargoyle's newest arrival, a brightly lit machine called *Wander*.

A dark-skinned boy wearing a T-shirt and shorts stood in front of the console, mashing buttons and splitting his time between playing and repeatedly checking his phone. *Wander* required the boy to weave his character through a three-dimensional haunted house, solving puzzles, while pressing a button that would zap an encroaching ghost. Each time a ghost appeared, the boy instinctively slammed his hand down on the button, sometimes without glancing up from his phone screen.

Two kids stood behind him. One of them, a stocky boy, about fourteen years old, shot the scene with an expensive piece of film equipment, while the other, a taller girl wearing bright orange lip gloss, beamed at the camera and spoke into a microphone.

"This is Rainy Riddle, of *Riddle Me Up a Storm,* reporting live at the Giggling Gargoyle Arcade. And as you can see just over my shoulder"—the girl scooted to one side to give her cameraman a better angle—"the legendary Devin Drobbs is at it again." She softly nudged Devin with her elbow. "Hey, Devin, looks like you're about to break another record."

Devin offered the girl a smug grin. "You think so? I hadn't really noticed."

Rainy giggled. "I'm dying to know how many tokens you've had to spend before deciding to attempt to make history today."

"Actually, this is my first time ever playing." Devin glanced over from the monitor, winked at the camera, and then pressed the button once more, instantly zapping a yowling ghost. An awe-inspired murmur passed through the crowd of onlookers. Devin could hear them whispering, wondering how he could play so flawlessly when he hardly ever looked at the screen.

A large man with a graying goatee and a Bluetooth ear-

piece protruding from his left ear shouldered his way in between Devin and Rainy. "All right, kiddos. Devin doesn't have
time to entertain every wannabe reporter from here to To-
ledo. If you want an interview, you're going to need to make
an appointment." The man whipped out a business card from
his shirt pocket and handed it to Rainy.

Rainy scowled. "Excuse me, but our viewership just sur-
passed one hundred thousand subscribers on our YouTube
channel." She paused to bat her eyelashes at the camera. "Be
sure to click the 'subscribe' link at the bottom of your screen
to check out all our videos."

"How old are you, kid?" the man asked.

"Rainy's thirteen, Dad," Devin said from behind them.
"She's in like three of my classes."

"Thirteen? With one hundred thousand subscribers?
That's way more than you have." The man rapped his knuckle
lightly against the back of Devin's head. "How is it you didn't
tell me about her?"

Devin slammed his hand down on the button and oblit-
erated a pair of snarling phantoms as his character arrived at
the final level. Celebratory music chimed from the console,
and a hush settled throughout the arcade.

"Dan Drobbs?" Rainy asked, glancing down briefly at the
business card. "You're Devin's father?"

A flashing light triggered on Mr. Drobbs's earpiece, and
Devin watched his dad step away, absently bumping into

people as he listened to the voice on his phone. Mr. Drobbs stopped walking and hunched over, both hands covering his ears to better hear the messenger. "Tomorrow morning?" he asked. "Yes, of course. Wait. He'll be coming to my house? No, not a problem at all. That will be just fine. We'll be ready. Oh no, thank you, sir."

Devin's hand slipped off the button as his dad spun around, a toothy smile stretched across his face. The crowd let out a collective groan as mournful music played from the game console and a three-headed phantom devoured Devin's character, ending his record-breaking run.

Rainy Riddle gasped. "You were so close! What do you have to say to your disappointed fans?"

"Who was on the phone?" Devin asked.

Devin's dad curled his lower lip and pointed at his earpiece. "Who, that? Oh, it was no one important."

Once again the crowd groaned, a few of them smashing their drink cups to the carpeted floor. But Devin wasn't upset. He pumped his fist in celebration.

"I knew it!" Devin cheered, high-fiving his dad. "I had a *feeling* I'd win!"

CHAPTER 4

ALMOST NINE THOUSAND miles away from Beyond, California, twelve-year-old Nika Pushkin boarded a private jet in the Domodedovo airport in Moscow, Russia. Flanked by an entourage of headpiece-wearing agents, Nika took her usual seat in the middle of the plane, next to the window. Nika's grandfather, Mikel Pushkin, sat down beside her.

"Please fasten your seat belts, my dear," her grandfather instructed.

Nika didn't protest. She pulled and locked her shoulder straps into position, each metal clasp buckling with a distinct clang. She then eased her legs into the custom-fitted braces located beneath her seat. Nika hated the way they clung to her skin like two mammoth leeches. Her grandfather assisted with connecting her forehead strap, the most awkward-fitting piece of all her dreaded seat belts. The forehead strap was only a requirement during takeoff, and whenever there was turbulence, but it made Nika feel like she was some sort of insane criminal being transported to a maximum-security prison.

"There we go," her grandfather whispered. "Comfortable?"

She shifted her eyes as she gave him a sideways glare.

"Don't be that way, my *printsessa*. I'm not making you wear your mouth guard. Not yet, at least. And I have a special treat for you. Milk shakes!" He snapped his fingers, and one of the agents produced a large Styrofoam cup. "Your favorite is vanilla, am I wrong?"

Nika stared at the milk shake and felt her mouth water. "How am I supposed to drink it?"

Her grandfather snapped his fingers again, and this time, an agent placed a straw in his hand. "They're not too thick. But, please, do take small sips."

Milk shakes were Nika's favorite, especially vanilla, but she liked them ice-cold. Grandfather would never approve of her drinking any substance that wasn't at the appropriate temperature. Not too hot or too cold.

Once the jet had leveled to its cruising altitude, Grandfather Pushkin allowed Nika to undo her wrist, head, and shoulder straps. Then he moved to the front of the jet to speak with his pilots.

"I want to watch the video again," Nika said to one of the men resting in the seats across the aisle. She nodded to the console hanging from the ceiling of the jet and sucked the rest of her now-lukewarm milk shake into her mouth. The man pressed a button on his radio and whispered into the mouthpiece on his lapel.

"You work for me," Nika hissed, and jabbed her index finger once more toward the TV. "You work for me. Now, do as I say."

The black screen of the television brightened as the familiar face came into view—that of the man she had met in her grandfather's office in Chelyabinsk less than a week before.

"Nika Pushkin, once again, congratulations for winning our contest. We're so excited to have you on board," Doug Castleton spoke on the video. "I understand you or your grandfather may still have doubts about whether or not you can do this, but I want nothing more than to put your mind at ease, because your safety is our utmost concern."

As the video continued, the jet entered a patch of turbulence, and Nika's grandfather reappeared from the cockpit. He glanced up at the screen and furrowed his brow. "This is the tenth time you have watched this video. Why do you do this?"

"What would you have me watch? Cartoons?" she asked.

On the screen, Doug held a bright orange suit. "Each of our four participants will be wearing one of these." He stretched the suit in his hands for emphasis. "It's practically indestructible. It can even repel a bullet fired at close range, but that would never happen, of course."

"Nika, my dear, I can have my pilot take us home, and I'll buy you whatever you desire," Nika's grandfather insisted.

She shook her head. "There's nothing else I want."

"What about a stable? You've always dreamed of riding. I will purchase you one with the finest horses and private lessons for you."

Nika glanced up at him, her eyes narrowing. "You would let me ride a horse?"

"If it meant ending this ludicrous charade, yes. I would consider it."

She scoffed. "*Consider* it." Riding an actual horse had been a dream of hers, but her *Dedushka* was only bluffing. "No. This is what I want."

Her grandfather knelt next to her chair, his hand resting softly on hers. "Before your father passed away, I told him that I would never purposely put you into harm's way." He drew her focus away from the console. "You are getting older and your health, my *printsessa,* it continues to deteriorate. We know very little about this ride. How can this Doug Castleton ensure your safety? He can't, Nika. No one can."

"I believe him," Nika said, nodding at the television screen. "That uniform will keep my body protected."

"Plastic. It's just plastic!" His voice grew agitated.

"*Dedushka,* stop," she said softly. "We are not going home. I entered the contest because I wanted to win. And you promised me that you would allow it for my birthday." She pulled her straw from her empty cup and licked off the remaining liquid.

It had taken quite a good deal of persistence from Nika and Doug to convince her grandfather to let her go to Beyond, California. Mikel Pushkin fought mightily against it, but in the end, he couldn't go back on the promise he'd committed to for her thirteenth birthday. Whatever her heart desired, he would deliver. It was fortunate Mr. Castleton arrived when he did, as Nika was just about to request a hot-air balloon ride, something her grandfather had forbidden since the moment she first saw one flying over their estate in Chelyabinsk when she was only seven years old.

Her grandfather pursed his lips. "Nika, it makes no sense to—"

"And I don't want to be treated any differently from the other participants. I am to be the same."

"The same?" He shook his head sternly, but his eyes softened. "You don't understand the risk involved. It is my duty as your grandfather to warn the Castletons of what precautions need to be taken to ensure your safety."

"Yes, but no one else is to know of my secret." She shook the empty cup above her head and her grandfather plucked it from her hands. "Remember, *Dedushka,* for this weekend, I am not broken."

CHAPTER 5

IT WAS AFTER three in the morning when Harold Dippetts returned to the Adventure Machine testing facility. He had taken a short break to grab a bite to eat from Taco Snyders, the only restaurant still open in Beyond, California, at that hour, before hurrying back to work. It had been another long day, but a necessary one. The contest winners would be arriving by the end of the week, and Harold was trying to meet his deadline.

As he gripped the doorknob to his office, Harold felt an uncomfortable burbling in his enormous stomach. He dropped a couple of antacids into his cup of black coffee and watched the froth bubble to the top.

"I should've passed on that second smothered burrito,"

he mumbled to himself, before pushing the door open. What he wouldn't give for a real home-cooked meal. Until the Adventure Machine went live, Harold was resigned to the fact that his meals would mostly consist of Taco Snyders burritos.

Harold blew across the lip of the paper cup and took a timid sip before spilling most of the liquid down the front of his shirt. He hadn't expected to see anyone in the office, and the sight of the man thumbing through Harold's workbook had startled him.

"Hello, Harold. How was your dinner?" It was Terry Castleton, Doug's older brother and the head of research and development at the Adventure Machine facility.

"Um—uh—I had burritos," Harold stammered, suddenly aware of a patch of dried hot sauce coating his chin.

Terry frowned at the crumpled bag gripped in Harold's hand. "From Taco Snyders? Why didn't you get something from the on-site cafeteria or the food court?"

Harold scrubbed nervously at the hot sauce with the sleeve of his lab coat. "Well, I think the cafeteria closes at nine, sir. Plus, I'm usually the only one in at this hour."

Terry smiled. "You're not the *only* one."

There were almost always two vehicles parked at the facility at all hours of the night: Harold's faded blue pickup truck (minus all four hubcaps), and Terry Castleton's silver Volvo.

Harold cleared his throat. "Not to sound rude or anything, but what . . . uh, what—"

"What am I doing in your office?" Terry asked. He closed the workbook and placed it on the desk. "I received word that you were close to finishing, and I wanted to take a look for myself."

Harold nodded and looked at the clock dangling crookedly from a peg above his desk. "What, you mean now?"

Terry moved toward the entrance of the lab at the back of Harold's office.

"If you don't mind. With the launch taking place this weekend, I need to make sure everything is set before our visitor arrives."

"Visitor? I was told there would be four participants."

"Yes, yes, there will be four, but I wasn't talking about the children. We have a very important member of the CTPAB witnessing the launch."

Harold dabbed the spilled coffee from his shirt with a napkin. "Oh yeah, I did hear that one of them would be coming." Of course. A lawyer from the California Theme Park Approval Board needed to give their final endorsement before the ride could be cleared for public access. Everything depended on that approval. Thus the need for Harold to work a month straight of sixteen-hour shifts.

"There's still a bunch of procedures to run through," Harold said, tossing his half-drank cup of coffee into the trash and hurrying to follow Mr. Castleton through the door. "It's just that—ouch . . ." Harold jarred the corner of his desk with his hip, sending half his collection of lizard action figures scattering across the floor. He furiously rubbed his side and fumed exhaustedly at the mess of lizards. He had barely finished posing them! "It's just that I'm not quite there yet."

They entered an expansive room with a lofty ceiling and pale white fluorescent light fixtures filling the area with a muted glow. Half a dozen contraptions that looked like massive metallic beehives occupied the space. A web of wires and tubes flowed out from the six-foot-tall machines and into a computer at the center of the room. Each of the hives had an amber bulb protruding from the top and a dark glass window at eye level.

"I've been meaning to ask you about the children," Harold said, watching apprehensively as Mr. Castleton circled one of the hives. "Will I be given a chance to meet them?"

Mr. Castleton stooped and examined a control panel. "Of course, Harold. I'll arrange for it."

Harold grimaced. "I . . . uh was wondering if I could possibly meet them before the launch?"

Terry stood and faced Harold, his expression stoic, unreadable. "Why would you need to meet them prior to the launch?"

Harold wiped the sweat from his cheek, wondering if he had asked too much. "For research purposes. These programs, as you know, are tricky, and I would like to make sure the ride does what it's supposed to do."

"I'm afraid that won't be possible," Terry said. "My brother will be entertaining the children in meetings and debriefings and all the necessities that go along with such an important event."

"It would just take a minute or two. A quick interview. A few questions."

Terry shook his head. "I'm sorry, Harold. I'm not about to ask my brother to break from his planned routine. That's what he does best, and it's his company. We all just work for him."

Harold realized that he had been holding his breath, and he exhaled a gust of air. "Well . . . um . . ."

"Now, could you please show me one?" Terry gestured to the hive.

Harold typed in his access code, breathing heavily as he studied the data that appeared on the screen. "They're not ready. I still need time to work out the kinks."

"Show me," Mr. Castleton said.

Harold pointed to one of the amber lights. "But sir, they're in hibernation."

Mr. Castleton pressed a fist against his lips and closed his eyes. "It's okay, Harold. Wake one of them up."

Harold's shoulders slumped. "I'll bring Pod One online."

Terry approached the closest machine to the entry door. He waited for Harold to give the signal and then peered through the glass. The buzzing in the room grew louder as power surged into the pod. There was a moment during which he said nothing. Then Harold heard Terry slowly exhale.

"Now," Terry said. "That, my friend, is fine work."

Harold felt his chest swell with pride. "You like it?"

"And they'll perform as commanded?" Terry asked.

"I think so, but like I said before, I need a little more time to test them together in a group. It's hard to determine which one will step forward as the leader, although I think it will be Pod One. He's more sophisticated than the others." Harold stared at his hands, which had taken on a slight tremor, before typing a string of commands on his keyboard. The image from inside the pod projected onto his monitor.

"It's beautiful, Harold. Perfect. We couldn't have asked for a better specimen."

On his screen, Harold watched as the man-sized creature inside the machine stood up and pressed one of its three-fingered claws against the glass.

CHAPTER 6

TREVOR SAT ACROSS from his mom in the back of a stretch limousine. The Isaacses had never ridden in a limo before, and they were enjoying the luxury vehicle. Well, Trevor was enjoying himself. His mom kept staring at the crumpled copy of the contract and mumbling about how she wished she could afford a lawyer.

"How am I supposed to know what all this mumbo jumbo means?" she asked.

Cold air flowed from the miniature refrigerator beneath the limo's privacy window as Trevor pulled out a corked bottle. "What's this?"

"That's champagne. Please put it back," his mom said. "And why aren't you wearing your seat belt?"

Trevor returned the bottle to its shelf and discovered a small plastic container of unusual-looking paste with a label listing a name he didn't recognize. He peeled open the lid, and a strong fishy scent wafted out of the opening. "What's caviar?"

"Fish eggs."

Trevor made a gagging noise, shut the lid, and tossed the container over his shoulder.

"Seriously?" His mom raised her voice. "We don't toss food on the floor."

"I didn't know it was food." Trevor picked up the fish eggs and placed them back in the refrigerator. "I thought it was bait."

The limo lurched as the driver took the exit off the freeway, and Trevor lost his balance. He fell backward and landed sharply on his rear end.

"Seat belt, now!" his mom ordered.

"All right, all right." Trevor plopped down in the seat and clicked his belt into place. "Why do I have to wear a seat belt in a car that has a couch and a refrigerator? That makes no sense."

"There will most likely be some hidden clauses in this thing that will break the whole contract. There always is. People just don't hand out an all-expenses-paid trip to California"—his mom hesitated, her eyes flitting to the back of the driver's head, before she lowered her voice—"and two hundred thousand dollars, without some sort of catch!"

"It's a contest, remember? It's like winning the lottery. These guys probably hand out money like that all the time," Trevor said. "They're super rich."

"And irresponsible!" Trevor's mom had been catching up on the hundreds of YouTube videos of Doug Castleton performing all sorts of dangerous stunts.

The limousine slowed, and the privacy window separating the front of the vehicle from the back opened a crack. "We've arrived." The driver pointed through the windshield at the building on the side of a sloping hill. Palm trees stood guard along the driveway, like dreadlocked soldiers.

"What the—" Trevor pushed his way through the privacy window to get a better look, surprising the driver, who nearly steered the limo off the road.

Trevor's mom tugged on the back of his shirt. "Sit down!"

The Adventure Machine facility wasn't anything like what Trevor had expected. Instead of looking like a theme park, with ticket booths leading into an open area where twisting metal roller coaster tracks spiraled in the background, there was a single massive building with multiple levels resting on the lawn. It looked like the sort of manor one would see on a Southern estate, complete with gaudy, cream-colored columns. Expansive windows glittered as spotlights lit up the building's facade. But what caught Trevor's eye was an enormous silver dome that loomed behind the building. Made of some kind of reflective material, the dome looked like a metal mountain. Trevor squinted, trying to see all the way to the top.

"What *is* that thing?" Trevor asked the driver.

"I just drive the car, buddy. Do you want to get back in your seat so I can pull up?"

Trevor sank into the cushion, the leather squeaking beneath him. "Mom, it's bigger than a stadium. No, two stadiums. Maybe even—"

"I can see it, honey," she said, stealing glances at the dome between rereading lines of text in the contract. "And, oh my word, what's with all the cameras?"

At least a dozen sharply dressed men and women stood behind velvety stanchions on the curb, pointing their video equipment at the approaching limousine. As soon as the limo pulled to a stop in front of the entryway, the passenger door was flung open, and Doug Castleton greeted them. Dressed in a Hawaiian shirt, khaki shorts, and flip-flops, Doug looked more like a beach bum ready to catch some waves than the owner and operator of an expensive theme park.

"So, what do you think?" Doug held out his hands to showcase the property. "Spectacular?"

"It's huge!" Trevor exclaimed. "How big is that thing?"

A barrage of flashes exploded from the rows of cameras. For just a moment, Trevor thought this must be what it felt like to arrive at a fancy movie premiere. Only there was no red carpet, there were no movie stars Trevor could see, and he was pretty sure he had sat in some gum on the airplane.

Doug put on a serious expression and lowered his voice. "Here, allow me to recite my lines," he said, before raising his voice. "'The Globe is four and a half million square feet and covers one hundred acres of land. It is the largest enclosed stadium-like structure in the world. It's five hundred and thirteen feet tall, and measures one thousand two hundred and twenty feet from end to end.'" He gave an exaggerated exhale, then offered his hand to assist Ms. Isaacs out of the limo. "Okay, let's take a couple of quick pics with the local media, and then I'll have Felix take your luggage to your room."

Trevor climbed out, glancing over his shoulder. "Who's Felix?"

The driver promptly saluted and then heaved the large suitcase out from the trunk.

Doug smiled at the wall of cameras, and Trevor shielded his eyes as another bombardment of flashes lit up the darkening evening sky. Several reporters vied for Trevor's attention, shouting questions and vigorously waving him over for an interview.

"Sorry, folks," Doug said. "Just pictures for now. We'll have plenty of time for some one-on-one discussions tomorrow, after the launch."

"Tomorrow?" Ms. Isaacs asked. "Who said anything about television interviews?"

"It's all outlined in your contract, Patricia," Doug said.

Trevor's mom snatched the contract from her purse and growled. "Oh really? And what page might that be on? Four hundred and seventy?"

Beyond the doors, Trevor expected to see a spiral staircase or a foyer with lounging couches and a grand piano, the customary furniture one would find in an uppity mansion. Instead, the building opened up into high, vaulted ceilings made almost entirely of glass, allowing full visibility of the mountainous Globe looming outside. Three Jumbotron-like movie screens hovered in the air, displaying a barrage of information with colorful images and booming audio.

As the sliding doors sealed shut behind Trevor, blocking out the cameras and the desperate voices of the news reporters, Doug gestured to the center of the atrium, where three children and their guardians stood waiting.

"Patricia and Trevor Isaacs, allow me to introduce you to Devin Drobbs and his father, Dan." Doug motioned to a dark-skinned boy standing with his arms folded. He had brown eyes and wore a red T-shirt and white basketball shorts. Devin held Trevor's gaze for a moment, before flicking his chin in acknowledgment. The boy's dad was an overly smiley fellow with a dark gray goatee. He brandished his phone in front of him and whispered something into his son's ear. Devin turned and flashed a confident grin, and Trevor realized that Mr. Drobbs was using his phone as a video camera.

"I thought we agreed we wouldn't be filming during this exchange," Doug said, pointing at Mr. Drobbs's device.

"Does the contract say not to?" Mr. Drobbs asked.

"Actually, it may—"

"Either it does or it doesn't, sir. And until a statement is noted in the fine print, I must insist on keeping my camera rolling." Mr. Drobbs took a step closer, zooming his camera in so he could capture Trevor's expression. "Little Rainy Riddle has one hundred thousand subscribers, eh, Devin?" He chuckled. "Well, we'll see who has more after this weekend."

"Moving on," Doug said, nodding to the next participant. "Nika Pushkin and her grandfather Mikel. They traveled all the way from Russia to join in the fun."

Though tall and skinny, Nika looked just around Trevor's age. She had straight brown hair, olive-colored skin, and wore a white long-sleeved shirt and blue jeans. The girl carried a paper cup from which she scooped ice cream with a spoon. Trevor thought she was kind of pretty, despite the fact that she appeared to be glowering at him. Beside her, a white-haired gentleman stood stoically, wearing a red sports coat.

"From Russia, huh?" Trevor asked.

"Yes," Nika answered. "We come from Chelyabinsk." Trevor could pick up only a slight hint of a Russian accent when she spoke.

"That must have been a long flight," he said. "We only had to fly in from Illinois."

Nika's grandfather sniffed and tugged on his sports coat lapels. "Fifteen-hour flight. Is not bad." Mr. Pushkin's accent came out thick and gruff, and he seemed incapable of smiling.

"Yeah, maybe not for you," Nika mumbled.

"What did they serve you to eat?" Trevor asked. Fifteen hours most likely required several meals.

Nika stared at Trevor warily, before glancing at the others in the foyer. "Milk shakes," she said, shaking her paper cup.

Doug nodded. "Right. And lastly, here are—"

"My name's Cameron," the third participant offered. He was a boy with thick red glasses that magnified his unblinking eyes, and stark blond hair parted down the middle. "Cameron Kiffing. It sounds like kissing, which I've never done, only instead there are Fs, which I've never earned. Presently, I'm the world's smartest eleven-year-old. My IQ is ten points above genius level. This is my mom. Her name's Beatrice. You can call her Ms. Kiffing, if you prefer." He nodded at the woman at his side. Ms. Kiffing was much shorter than the other adults, and she possessed a bewildered, almost lost expression, as though she had no recollection of how she had arrived at the Adventure Machine facility.

"World's smartest eleven-year-old?" Trevor asked. "I don't even know what my IQ is, but I'm not afraid of kissing girls or getting Fs." Not that he had done either, but at least he could safely say he wasn't afraid. Trevor's mom swatted his arm.

Devin snickered and whispered something under his breath to his dad. Nika glanced up from her milk shake and looked at Trevor, the faintest hint of a smile forming on her lips.

Cameron cocked his head to the side to study Trevor as well. "Strictly by my unprofessional opinion, I would have to say you have an IQ of 110, 115 tops."

"Is that good?" Trevor asked.

Cameron shrugged halfheartedly. "Meh."

"This is it. This is our crew," Doug said. "And we are on the eve of your grand adventure. Now, if you will turn your attention up—" Doug gestured to the ceiling above them and the lights in the atrium dimmed. The informational displays on the Jumbotrons disappeared. Lasers shot out from the center of each of the three screens, converging into one massive beam that reached all the way to the floor. The beam appeared distorted at first, but then it grew solid, forming a door. Trevor applauded and glanced at the other winners. They all seemed equally mesmerized by the awesome display.

Suddenly, the three-dimensional image of a man appeared, emerging from the cylindrical door. If Trevor hadn't known better, he would've believed the man to be actually standing there in front of them; it was that flawless. The only proof otherwise was a few granulated pixels.

"Hello, lucky winners," the holographic man said. "My name is Terry Castleton." He had thinning gray hair and a few wrinkles weaving out from the corners of his mouth, but there was no mistaking the striking similarities to Doug. They both had the same eyes and the same confident smile. "I'm head of research and development at the Adventure Machine facility, and I'm here today to show you our most *prized* creation." More lasers, a fraction of the size of the center beam, zigzagged down from the Jumbotrons, dancing across the ground. Like magic erasers, the lasers replaced a circular section of marble floor with bubbling lava. Trevor heard someone gasp. Devin and his dad took a cautious step back from the display. It wasn't real, of course. Just an impressive show, but Trevor thought he could feel actual heat emanating from the virtual lava.

"My brother, Terry, would've been here himself," Doug whispered to the group as the lasers continued transforming the ground into a volcanic landscape. "But unfortunately, he had a few meetings to attend. He'll be here tomorrow for the launch."

The lasers finished their work, leaving only a tiny rock beneath Terry's feet.

"You are about to embark on the adventure of a lifetime," Terry said, then he vanished and was replaced by a long, silver vehicle. It looked like a standard roller coaster cart with an aerodynamic cone, four cushioned seats, and thick safety harnesses that pulled down over riders' shoulders. Trevor had seen similar ones before and had even ridden in a few prior to being permanently banned from every amusement park in Illinois. Apparently, people didn't like it when you got out of your seat during the ride. Who knew?

"We call it the Adventure Machine." Terry's disembodied voice spoke as the image of the roller coaster rotated, giving the group the ability to view the contraption at all angles. The cart then began moving forward along a track. "Using state-of-the-art technology, the Adventure Machine taps into the riders' minds to create a thrilling experience."

The background blurred as the vehicle reached incredible speeds. It plummeted down steep slopes, careered through loops, bucked, pitched, and barrel-rolled, before screeching to a stop.

"Imagine a ride that will allow you to experience this." A series of intense scenes flashed across the screen. The cart surged through a fire-filled landscape. There was a blinding blizzard, followed by an avalanche and a tidal wave; then the images flipped through countless other scenarios, before ending with a final scene of the cart vanishing into a pitch-black tunnel.

The column of light vanished along with the Adventure Machine and Terry Castleton. The Jumbotrons once again displayed their previous images.

"What do you think?" Doug asked, once the transmission had ended.

"I don't understand how you can do this," Devin's dad said. "A roller coaster track has to be sturdy and rigid. How can you manipulate the landscape so freely?"

"And what exactly should our children expect to encounter on this ride?" Cameron's mom asked. She stood, arms folded, scowling at the Jumbotrons as though she could still see the remnants of the Adventure Machine transmission. "Was that actual lava?"

Doug rubbed his hands together. "We use a new technology that allows the riders to have an entirely out-of-body experience."

Trevor frowned. "So it's not real, then?"

"Oh, it's real," Doug said. "That's the beauty of it. You think you're in for an ordinary ride and then the Adventure Machine jumps up and smacks you right in the mouth."

Trevor's mom anxiously tapped her toe. "Okay, I just have to ask: Why do we need a contract for this?"

"Yeah," Devin's dad said. "What are we agreeing to?"

"You're agreeing to allow your child to ride the Adventure Machine, of course," Doug answered matter-of-factly.

"You're going to make every person who wants to ride your roller coaster sign a contract?" Ms. Kiffing asked.

"Oh no, not at all. Once the Adventure Machine goes public, anyone who buys a ticket will have all access to the ride. The contract is just for you."

Trevor's mom narrowed her eyes. "So that we don't sue you when my son loses his arm during an accident, am I right?"

Doug smiled sheepishly and stared at the ceiling. "That's a bit extreme, but I guess the contract does cover some liabilities."

"Contracts? Liabilities? Lava? We need some answers now. Don't you think?" Trevor's mom demanded. The other parents grumbled their consent.

Doug pressed his hands together, steepling his fingers beneath his chin. "And you'll have them. If you'll follow me, we'll now head to our legal offices to discuss all this. Every question will be answered. I assure you."

"Great!" Trevor said sarcastically. "Legal offices sound like a really fun time." He glanced around at the others. Devin pretended to yawn. "Do we all get to go?" Trevor asked.

"Hey, I have a great idea," Doug said. "Since us adults have to wander off and attend to boring contract business, there's no reason for the kids to tag along. Should we allow our lucky winners the chance to stretch their legs and explore?" He flourished his hand toward the far side of the atrium.

Flickering lights embedded in the floor illuminated a path weaving toward a massive mouth. Trevor smirked at the sight of the jagged teeth and fat red lips surrounding the entrance. Even the carpet had been designed to look like a tongue. The words *The Gallery* glowed in neon above it.

"The Gallery is a discovery zone," Doug explained. "A way for you, the ticket holder, to get a feel for what you're about to experience. The main attraction in the Gallery, of course, is our Terrorarium."

"So is it like a museum?" Trevor asked, glancing uneasily over at his mom. The bill for Trevor's unplanned crash landing had arrived from the East Chester Museum just the day before, forcing Trevor to relive the incident all over again.

"Sort of," Doug said. "You'll find things on display there that can't be explained. There are games and booths and interactive adventures that perhaps will give a face to your nightmares. Think of it as a freak show."

"And they have a food court too," Cameron added.

Doug grinned. "That's right, Cameron. Did you wander off by yourself earlier?"

Cameron's eyes widened slightly. "Of course not, but I

did do a little exploring of your facilities online prior to our arrival this afternoon."

Trevor's eyes lit up as his stomach gurgled. "Food court? In there?" He jabbed his index finger emphatically at the mouth.

"Most of it is nonfunctioning at the moment, but I've asked a few of the tenants to be on-site for this special weekend," Doug said. "I think we have Samurai Sal's Sushi, Bortho's Burgers, and some vegan restaurant, but I always forget its name. When all's said and done, we'll have twenty different restaurants and three gift shops."

"What about the Adventure Machine?" Trevor asked. "When are we going to see that?"

"Yeah, isn't that the whole point of the contest?" Devin added. "Let's take a look at that bad boy."

"Patience, my friends. All in due time. We'll get you there in the morning," Doug said. "What do you say, Moms, Dad, Grandpa? Should we allow the kiddos to take their leave?"

Devin glanced at his dad, who nodded in agreement. "That sounds cool. You said there are games?"

Doug nodded. "Pretty sure most of them you've never heard of."

"Are you really good at video games?" Nika asked Devin.

Devin waggled his eyebrows. "If you want, you can follow me and I'll show you how good I am."

Mikel Pushkin gently placed his hands on his grand-daughter's shoulders. "Nika will not be joining you this evening."

Nika closed her eyes in disappointment. "But, *Dedushka,* couldn't I—"

"Absolutely not," Mikel said, never looking down at her. "Thank you for your hospitality, Mr. Castleton, but I've al-ready signed the contract and I trust you will honor our ar-rangement by keeping my granddaughter completely safe. We will take our dinner in our room. Good night." He guided Nika away from the group, and they headed off toward the elevators.

Trevor watched them leave, noticing how Nika's grand-father moved out in front of her as they walked, guiding her away from the walls and any other obstacles that arose in their path. Nika glanced back at the group longingly, before turning and tossing her empty milk shake cup into one of the garbage receptacles.

Cameron looked pleadingly at his mother. "Can I go?"

Ms. Kiffing cupped her hand over her mouth. "Did you take your pill?"

"Shhh, Mom! Of course I did!" he hissed. "Who wants to go with me to the museum?" he asked in a louder voice.

Ms. Isaacs folded her arms and looked at Trevor. "I don't know. I don't like the idea of separating from you in such a strange place."

"Come on, Mom," Trevor begged. "I'm starving." There may have been a meal offered on the flight, but it was soggy, steamed vegetables and something that might have been gelatinized pork. "I promise I'll stay right in there."

Trevor's mom's looked skeptical. "You don't expect me to believe that, do you?"

"There's plenty to keep him occupied," Doug chimed in. "The rest of the building is just a hotel, some offices, a few maintenance closets, a medical clinic. All basically shut down until we're operational. Wouldn't be much fun for him to go wander around, while there's a whole world of weird just past the tonsils." He flicked his chin at Trevor and winked. "Go on, Trev. You have an all-access pass this weekend. Have fun, explore, and grab one of Bortho's signature cheeseburgers while you're at it. It will knock your socks off!"

Oh yeah. Trevor's eyes widened. A sock-knocking cheeseburger was definitely called for.

Trevor's mom stacked the contract in a neat pile. "I suppose you could go."

Before she could throw out another stipulation, Trevor bolted for the Gallery. He could faintly hear his mom shouting not to run, but the sound of his sprinting feet drowned out her voice. Then he was racing up the tongue, and the mouth swallowed him whole.

CHAPTER 7

TWO THICK PATTIES of beef topped with three strips of crispy bacon and melted American cheese oozed on one half of a buttered bun. Trevor slathered mayonnaise on the other half before squishing it on top. The juices dripped over his plate of French fries. If this burger tasted even half as good as it looked or smelled, Bortho's Burgers would become Trevor's new favorite restaurant.

Aside from a few employees at Bortho's, Samurai Sal's, and Beets & Weeds, the vegan restaurant, Trevor had the whole food court to himself. Gripping the burger with both hands, he raised it to his lips, then hesitated.

Cameron Kiffing had somehow magically appeared at

one of the circular tables next to a fountain, and he was intently watching Trevor eat.

"Where did you come from?" Trevor asked.

"Pennsylvania. Ardmore City," Cameron said, picking up a chopstick and fumbling as he thumb wrestled a piece of sushi. He pushed his glasses farther up his nose with the knuckle of his index finger, before finally giving up on the sushi and surrendering a rapid blink. "You have what scientists call a misfiring amygdala, which makes you devoid of feeling any fear."

Trevor lowered his burger from his mouth, and a glob of hot cheese dripped onto his plate. "How do you know that?"

"I read it." The sound of a carbonated can opening rang out in the food court, and Cameron pulled a tall energy drink from his lap and placed it on the table.

"You read it?" How was he able to read about Trevor's condition? Did that mean they all could? It was supposed to be confidential. "Look, I don't want anyone to know about that."

"Your secret's safe with me!" Cameron hopped up from his seat and scurried over to where Trevor was sitting. The boy's short legs dangled from the chair. "I have a secret too. I've been diagnosed with a rare case of hyperactive ingenuity, which means that I'm really smart and sometimes out of control."

"I don't know if that's necessarily a secret," Trevor said, grinning.

Cameron offered Trevor his drink. "Kraken Spit?"

"No thanks." Trevor noticed the snarling octopus-like monster on the side of the dark blue can.

"I like the taste of Kraken Spit," Cameron said, examining the drink thoughtfully. "It's more agreeable with my palate than other enhanced stimulant-inducing beverages, and it fails to cause any of the typical side effects, such as the jitters. My parents don't approve of me consuming these drinks, as they tend to elevate my hyperactivity, and then I end up mostly naked."

"Naked?" Trevor scrunched his nose.

"Mostly naked," Cameron said. "When my mind needs to be free to solve, so does the rest of me, I suppose."

Trevor was having a hard time keeping up with Cameron. He had never met a boy so willing to share things of a personal nature with complete strangers. Plus, the kid talked as fast as an auctioneer. "So are you just going to sit there and watch me eat?"

"I can, if you want. And then afterward, we could go to the Museum of Freaks together."

"Look, no offense, but I don't think I want to go to some museum." Trevor stole a piece of bacon from beneath the bun and slipped it into his mouth. It was crispy, greasy, and perfect. But the burger was definitely getting cold.

"Why?" Cameron asked. "You don't appreciate knowledge?"

"It's not that." Well, maybe it was a little. "I'm not here to learn stuff. I'm here to ride the Adventure Machine. That's the whole point, right? Now, if you could tell me where to find—"

"I think it's downstairs." Cameron slurped, muffled a belch, and cleared his throat.

"What's downstairs?"

"Something important. I downloaded the floor plans of this place, and there's something definitely big on the bottom floor. I doubt it's the entrance to the Globe, mind you. That will most likely be heavily monitored, and one would only have access through a specific entrance. But I noticed a few interesting notes signaling some sort of factory or warehouse on the lowest level. My guess is that's where they built the machine."

"Okay, slow down," Trevor said. "Are you saying there may be a way to check out the Adventure Machine through the elevators?"

Cameron nodded.

"Do you want to go down there with me?" Trevor asked.

Cameron's eyes widened, and he shook his head. "I'd rather go to the Museum of Freaks. There's supposed to be a whole horde of strange-looking taxidermied creatures on display. Two-headed lizards, winged goats, apes. Most likely all fake, but interesting nonetheless."

"Sounds fun," Trevor said, getting up.

"You're not really going downstairs, are you?" Cameron asked. "Because there are probably strict rules about venturing into those parts of the facility."

"I was just curious." Trevor sat back down.

"You could breach your contract. Get arrested!"

"Settle down. I'm not going anywhere." *At least not while everyone's awake and wandering around.*

Trevor smiled and took a gigantic bite of his burger. The juices from the beef and melted cheese exploded down his chin and dripped onto the collar of his shirt. He wiped his mouth with the back of his arm and moaned in satisfaction. For a moment, he imagined he could feel his socks preparing to launch from his feet.

CHAPTER 8

THERE WAS NO doubt in Devin's mind that sneaking out of his bedroom that night was a bad idea. His actions would land him in a world of trouble, and it didn't take his acute sense of anticipation to know that. It wasn't a matter of *if* he would get caught; it was a matter of when.

Devin knew this, but he didn't care. At that very moment, he had a tingly feeling that one of the other participants was out of bed as well. Across the room, Devin's dad stirred. He grumbled something incoherent, smacked his lips, and then resumed disrupting the silence with his thunderous snoring, a black Batman blindfold covering his eyes.

Devin slipped his phone into his pocket, quietly opened the door, and crept out into the dimly lit hallway. He hurriedly walked by the Pushkins' room, and then paused as he approached the Isaacses'. Devin felt a vibration in his chest, and he closed his eyes, trying to concentrate.

"What a punk," he whispered. No way was he going to let Trevor explore the facility all by himself. Devin didn't know much about him, but Trevor definitely gave off a curiosity vibe like no other.

When he arrived at the end of the hall, in front of the door leading into the Kiffings' room, Devin quieted his footsteps. Waking up Cameron Kiffing would be a disaster. That annoying kid had already cornered Devin once, forcing him into a conversation he didn't want to have. How could Cameron have known about his intuitions, his *feelings*?

Devin stepped into the elevator and studied the assortment of buttons. It was at that point that he noticed the blinking security camera nestled in the upper corner of the elevator.

"You've got to be kidding me!"

Of course there would be a camera. Why hadn't he thought of that? Devin wondered who might be watching him at that hour, but his tingling had gone soft.

Oh well, he thought. *No point in going back now.* The damage had been done. Devin smiled at the camera and then pretended to pick his nose, just for fun. When the doors opened at the bottom floor, he plowed face-first into Trevor.

Trevor backed up in surprise. "It's Devin, right? What are you doing down here?"

"Maybe I should be asking *you* the same question." Devin pulled his phone out of his pocket and pressed record on the camera. Devin's dad had lectured him about wasting hours of footage on the mundane details of his daily routine. Bumping into Trevor, however, was definitely worth filming.

"So, here I was, minding my own business . . . ," Devin said into his phone, before turning the camera on Trevor. ". . . when I discovered this guy wandering around in the restricted area of the facility."

Trevor blinked innocently. "Restricted? Who said anything about it being restricted?"

"I wonder what Doug would think of this information?" Devin continued, zooming in on Trevor's obnoxious grin. "Would he be upset? Would Trevor land himself in hot water?"

"Are you taping me right now?"

Devin nodded, a smile etching itself across his face. "This is going to be featured on my new YouTube channel under the heading 'Devin catches the sneak and sends him packing home without his prize money.'"

Trevor rolled his eyes. "That sounds like a really exciting video. Remind me to check it out when I get home after I ride the Adventure Machine."

"My YouTube channel is going to blow up after our big

ride tomorrow. I'll probably have like a million subscribers by the end of next week." So far, Devin had only managed to add two hundred subscribers to his measly fifty, piggy-backing off Rainy Riddle's latest arcade video. But Devin was bound for greatness. At least, that was what his dad told him.

"I'm going to be famous, dude. And maybe you'll be famous too," Devin said. "Famous for getting caught on tape robbing the Adventure Machine facility."

"Have fun with that." Trevor tried to shoulder past, but Devin held up his hand.

"Relax. I'm only kidding," he said. "I'm not going to tell anyone about this. And if I do post the footage, I'll blur your face out so no one knows who you are."

"Really don't care if you do," Trevor said, but he stopped trying to force his way into the elevator. "So, when did you talk to your best pal, Cameron?"

Devin hit the pause button on his camera. "Talk to him about what?" If that Cameron said anything to Trevor . . .

"About me sneaking down here," Trevor said. "I knew it was a bad move, inviting him to tag along. He freaked out about it earlier."

Devin felt relief swimming in his chest. He studied Trevor's eyes for a moment and then rolled his shoulders. "I didn't talk to that goob, and he's not my best pal."

"Then how did you know I was coming?"

"You just looked like someone who would."

Trevor shrugged. "What's your problem with Cameron anyway?"

"He's a little know-it-all who won't last a minute on the Adventure Machine." The first part of that was absolutely true. Devin had met many know-it-alls in his day—psychiatrists, doctors, and scientists—but Cameron took first prize in that contest. Devin didn't know exactly how long Cameron would last on the ride; his gift didn't work that way. But judging by Cameron's timid demeanor, that kid was destined to freak out the moment the cart took off down the track.

"What about Nika?" Trevor asked. "She seems pretty cool."

Devin snickered. "You just said she was pretty."

"No, I said she was pretty cool."

"Forget about it, dude. She's totally got the hots for me. You heard her when she practically begged to follow me into the arcade."

Trevor groaned, but Devin playfully slugged him in the shoulder. "Just kidding, dude. So how long have you been down here?"

Trevor glanced over his shoulder and nodded toward the end of the hallway. "Long enough to see some weird stuff. There's a kind of warehouse, and there's a guy working in his office right next to it, but he's not paying attention."

Devin swallowed, a slight tremor quivering in his chest. "Are you sure he's not paying attention?" Suddenly, he felt a completely different vibe from what Trevor had just described. Devin sensed that the man in the office knew full well what was up.

Trevor's eyes widened. "Come on. You've got to see it for yourself. It's pretty awesome."

Devin gawked at the oddly shaped machines as he stepped into the expansive warehouse-like room and eased the door closed behind him.

"Have you ever seen anything like them?" Trevor asked.

Devin shook his head and approached the first metal container, an almost pyramid-shaped machine, but with rounded edges, like a beehive. A gigantic beehive with glowing gold lights at the top. He placed his hand against the side of one of the machines and listened. "It's warm," he said. "And it's buzzing."

Trevor tapped a twelve-inch section of glass at eye level. "I think this is some sort of window."

Devin thought it looked more like a small television monitor than a window. The black glass revealed nothing beyond it, even when Devin pressed his face against it, cupping his hands around his eyes. At his feet, a mass of wires, like multicolored arteries, zigzagged away from each of the machines and connected to the back of a computer. Devin stepped over the wires and bumped the table. The monitor crackled as the dark screen began to brighten, and a series of numbers and words appeared.

Pod #1: Hibernating
Pod #2: Hibernating
Pod #3: Hibernating

It was the same for each of the six lines.

"Hibernating? What do you think that means?" Devin asked.

"Don't know, but I tried a whole bunch of password attempts to turn them on," Trevor said.

Devin smirked. "Wait, you're serious. How long were you in here before?"

Trevor gnawed on his lip. "Maybe half an hour. There's no way to open those things either." He pointed to one of the hives. "They're like locked or something."

Something flashed on the monitor, causing the boys to stare once more at the screen. The first line of text was now highlighted, and the wording had changed.

Pod #1: Activating

Devin backed away from the computer. "What did you touch?"

"Nothing," Trevor said, moving the cursor with the mouse. "It just did it by itself. I wonder which one's pod number one?"

The screen flashed once more, and the wording changed again.

Pod #1: Online

The gold light above the pod closest to the door turned bright green, and the glass window began to glow.

"Sweet!" Trevor exclaimed.

Devin eyed the door. "You're going to break something. Let's get out of here."

"You don't want to see what's inside?"

From his peripheral vision, Devin noticed a flicker of movement as a dark shadow filled the opening behind the glass. "I think I'll stay back here."

Trevor stepped toward the pod.

"What if it's radioactive? Hey! Are you listening to me?"

"Chill out, dude," Trevor said. "Let's just take a look."

"I don't want to take a look. I want to go back to my room." This had gone far enough. This was just supposed to be about some cool video footage. But Trevor was as stubborn as a mule. "What if you're not supposed to look directly . . ." His voice trailed off. Everything behind him in the room, the humming sounds of the other machines, the crackling whir of the computer, had all blurred together.

At that moment, Devin could only see the hideous face staring directly out from behind the glass.

CHAPTER 9

DEVIN'S FIRST THOUGHT was *Aliens*. Like the ones from a movie he had seen a few years ago. In fact, it felt as though he were watching a movie on a miniature screen, and witnessing the arrival of some intelligent being from another world. But there was no theater. Whatever this thing was, it had grown interested in Devin. It was blinking its bulbous yellow eyes at him.

Trevor pressed his face against the screen, completely blocking the creature from seeing out anymore. Devin felt a wave of relief. But how could Trevor be acting so reckless?

"Hey, man, have you ever seen *Morlock of Mars*?" Trevor asked, not pulling back from the glass.

"Yeah," Devin answered warily. "Why?"

"This thing kinda looks like Morlock. Only taller and uglier." He pounded on the pod with his fist, creating a dull, hollow thump.

"I'm going back to my room," Devin said. He was breathing rapidly now.

"Wait just a couple more minutes. I want to try to talk to it." Trevor drummed on the side of the pod. "Hey, Morlock, can you understand me?"

"It's not Morlock. And banging on that pod is no different than banging on an aquarium."

Trevor looked back, scrunching his eyebrows. "What's wrong with banging on an aquarium?" He brought his hand back, ready to pound once again, but stopped within inches of the metal. "Why are you still standing all the way over there? Are you scared or something?"

"I'm not scared!"

"Then take a look." Trevor moved to one side. "Don't you want good footage?"

Devin felt queasy. He had no desire to look inside now that it was occupied by that thing, but he couldn't let Trevor think he was afraid. He slowly approached the hive.

"It's not going to get you," Trevor said. "It's trapped inside."

"I know that!" Devin leaned forward and pressed his face against the glass.

The insect-like creature stood near the back of the pod, trying to stretch its limbs within the cramped confines. Tall and slender, with skin like black, polished leather, its shoulders would've skimmed the ceiling had it not been purposely bending its knees. It wore a solid piece of shimmering fabric draped down from its waist, which covered the majority of its lower body.

"Holy cow," Devin whispered. The creature cocked its head, as if curious, studying Devin as a snake might do with a small child gawking at it in a pet store. In an instant, Devin leapt back at least a foot, the warnings of a scream catching in his throat.

Trevor grinned, nudging Devin with his elbow. "He's a beast, huh?"

"Yeah, definitely." Devin moved backward away from the hive, his rear end bumping into the computer desk.

"Are you all right? You're shaking."

Devin scowled at Trevor. "I'm fine." But he wasn't fine. At that moment, Devin felt the worst kind of tingling in his chest, as if something bad was about to happen.

Trevor once again peered into the hive. "Geez, he's gotta be seven feet tall, don't you think?"

"Seven and a half," someone announced from the other side of the room.

Devin whirled around, clutching his hand against his

chest. A man with a pair of dark-rimmed glasses and a mustache stood in the open doorway. He was thin and wearing tan slacks and a button-up collared shirt.

"I—uh—I didn't touch anything," Devin stammered, sliding away from the computer.

"It's all right, Devin," the man said.

Devin's shoulders slumped. *He knows my name.* They were so busted!

"Hey, you're the guy from that virtual video Doug showed us earlier." Trevor glanced away from the window and snapped his fingers. "You're Doug's brother, Terry."

"That's correct," the man said, and then pointed to the hive next to Trevor. "So what do you think? Impressive, isn't he?"

"Oh yeah," Trevor said. "He's like the coolest thing I've ever seen. How did you make him?"

Terry Castleton walked casually into the room and approached the table where Devin stood trying to make himself invisible. "I can't take credit for him, though I did help some in the design. Relax, son, you're making me nervous with the way you're holding your breath."

Devin exhaled, puffing out his cheeks and eyeing the door. "We shouldn't have come down here. You're not going to send us home, are you?"

"Send you home without riding the Adventure Machine?" Terry clicked his tongue. "Not a chance. You've done nothing wrong. Have you taken the opportunity to look at One?"

"One what?" Devin asked, relieved to know he wasn't in trouble.

Terry stooped over the keyboard and typed a few commands into the computer. "There are six pods in all, and we label the creatures by their numbers. We're not too creative when we come up with names. That's the first pod, and that's One."

"We already met him," Trevor said, and he pounded a fist against the side of the machine. Instead of a resonating sound one might hear from a hollowed-out enclosure, the metallic pod produced a dull, heavy din. For the slightest of moments, the glass screen flickered, and the creature behind it looked almost pixelated.

"Careful, son," Terry said. "That's a fifteen-million-dollar piece of equipment you're pounding on, and the technology is entirely new. If you damage something, we wouldn't be able to find replacement parts for quite some time."

"Oh, sorry." Trevor gently patted the spot he'd struck, as if trying to soothe its wound.

"It's all part of the ride," Terry said. "When the Adventure Machine officially opens to the public, participants will be introduced to their adventure here first, in what we call the Habitat Room. Doug wants this to be one of the most intense moments of their whole adventure. Seeing the creatures and communicating with them in this setting will allow for a completely unique experience when they interact with them on the ride."

Devin felt the weight of his phone in his pocket and knew that he should've been filming this interaction with Terry and the creature. If his dad discovered he had missed out on some one-of-a-kind footage, he would flip. They could have uploaded the video as an exclusive, first-time look at the monsters of the Adventure Machine on their channel.

"It's late, boys. I think it's time you head back to your rooms," Terry said. "I would keep what you've seen here a secret until after you finish your adventure tomorrow. You two are lucky. The pods aren't planned to be part of your initial tour. The Habitat Room won't be live for a few more weeks. If the others discovered that you stole a free tour, they might see it as you receiving preferential treatment."

"I can keep a secret," Trevor said, glancing over at Devin.

"I doubt they'll care," Devin said. "Seeing that monster made me a little nervous, and I know it would've freaked the both of them out."

"A little nervous?" Trevor waggled his eyebrows. He stole another peek into the glass and then back at Terry. "Is One supposed to be looking at me like he wants to rip my face off?"

Terry shrugged. "He's programmed to create his own opinions about the participants, but I won't go into that anymore tonight. You two better get back before your parents discover you're missing," he said. "Get plenty of rest. Tomorrow the real fun begins."

CHAPTER 10

WHEN THE DOOR to the office burst open, Harold yelped and fell out of his chair. Cold coffee splattered across the linoleum from his overturned mug, and a wastebasket crammed with tubes of blueprints and other assorted papers toppled and scattered.

Both of the Castleton brothers stood in the doorway to Harold's office. Not just Terry, but also Doug Castleton, the owner of CastleCorp!

"As I'm sure you're aware by now, a couple of the ride participants have made an unscheduled visit to the laboratory," Terry Castleton said coolly.

"Ye . . . ah, about that. I, uh, wasn't sure what I should do. I suppose I could've alerted security, but it was so unexpected."

Harold reached over sideways and attempted to herd an array of pens and used plastic straws back into their holder on his desk. As if the pencils were the main eyesore in the room. Had a tornado suddenly formed and torn through the office, there would've been no difference. His eyes darted to the various piles of garbage sprouting up like gopher mounds.

"Harold, this is my brother, Doug," Terry said, gesturing with his palm. "I don't believe you two have met."

"Not officially." Doug clicked his tongue and winked. "I'm really only familiar with Harold's work, but I do also sign his checks."

"Can you show us what we've learned from this encounter?" Terry asked.

Plopping down in his chair, Harold scooted up to his desk. "You usually don't see a connection like this." He paused to catch his breath as he felt a hand press firmly on his shoulder, and glanced up to see the brothers hovering over his workstation. "Again, this is just, I mean, it's too soon to come to any firm conclusions, but—"

"Pull up the data, Harold," Terry instructed.

Harold's fingers clumsily navigated his keyboard, entering a series of commands, which produced a chart of numbers on the screen. Terry leaned closer, reading the data. Doug didn't appear to be as interested in the raw statistics as his older brother, but from what Harold knew of him, and that was based purely on Doug's YouTube channel, numbers and data weren't really his thing. Doug liked to jump out of airplanes without a parachute. No manner of statistics could ever convince Harold to pull off such a harebrained stunt.

Terry straightened and slid his glasses off his ears. "Fascinating. And all the children did was look through the screen."

"That's all it takes," Harold said. "The creatures have ocular reception."

"So you knew this would happen?" Terry asked, pointing to the screen.

Harold shook his head vehemently, but that morphed into a half nod. "It was only just earlier this morning that I completed the final programming." Not to mention the fact that Harold had made several rapid changes to the program right after he realized the two boys were about to sneak into the lab. But he wasn't about to reveal those changes to the Castletons. Harold wasn't that stupid.

Terry stared at Harold for several uncomfortable seconds. Finally, his gaze softened, and a smile cracked the stonelike surface of his expression.

"Brilliant, Harold. Absolutely brilliant!" he said. "That was a risky move, allowing the boys to enter the laboratory, one that could've jeopardized our entire launch. But I suppose risks are necessary for greatness to be achieved."

Doug cleared his throat, and Harold yelped for the second time that evening. He had completely forgotten that the other Castleton brother was even in the room.

"For the benefit of someone who has no idea what you're talking about, could you please explain what's going on?" Doug asked, then added, "In words I can understand."

Harold scratched the side of his head. He honestly had no clue what words Doug would be able to understand. Everything about the project used a vocabulary spoken only by geniuses, which the younger Castleton most certainly was not.

Terry gave Harold a solid pat on his shoulder. "The project is a success."

"Come on, Terry," Doug said, clear annoyance in his tone. "I may not be tech-savvy like you two, but I do pay the bills. And I don't think I need to remind you how much is riding on tomorrow's launch."

Terry chuckled. "And here I thought I was always the serious one. Relax, Doug. What else is there to know?"

"We're not jeopardizing these kids, right?" Doug pressed. "We're going to have four preteens strapped in to a ride that's never been tested before. Not to mention their guardians will be on-site watching the whole event transpire. I don't want to think about the legal ramifications if something goes wrong."

"I'm assuming you had legal clear you of any liability in the contract," Terry said.

"Of course." Doug winked at Harold. "It's buried so deep in the fine print you'd need a microscope to find it."

Harold grinned and pressed his fist against his mouth to stifle a belch.

"All joking aside, I just need to know that we're not putting our participants in any real danger," Doug said.

Terry returned his glasses to his inside suit coat pocket. "Well, that depends."

"Depends on what?" Doug asked.

"That depends on what you consider *real* danger to be."

CHAPTER 11

NIKA HAD ALMOST finished her breakfast when Trevor finally stumbled into the food court the next morning. She, along with the other kids and their guardians, sat at several circular tables grouped together near the center of the spacious room.

"Finally decided to join us, did you?" Nika asked Trevor as he pulled one of the chairs away from the table and sat down with an exhausted plop. "You're lucky we didn't leave without you." She polished off the last ounce of her orange juice.

"Yeah, it's about time," Ms. Isaacs said. "I tried dragging you out of bed over an hour ago. What's the deal, bucko?" She attacked an out-of-place shock of hair on the back of Trevor's head with her hand.

Trevor swatted her hand away. "What do I do to get breakfast?" He looked over at the restaurants, all of which were closed.

"The breakfast is catered, but you serve yourself." Cameron pointed across the floor to where two banquet tables held a variety of steaming chafing dishes. "They have French toast. I love French toast," Cameron said. "It's so good!"

"Do you eat it with a straw?" Trevor asked.

Nika giggled as she noticed Cameron's plate and his single slice of French toast doused with easily half a bottle of maple syrup. It looked more like a prehistoric insect buried in amber.

Cameron opened his mouth to respond, but Trevor was already weaving between chairs and tables on his way to the far side of the food court.

"Were you not able to sleep last night?" Nika asked when Trevor returned, balancing his toast on top of a mountain of eggs, sausage, and bacon.

"I was just up late thinking about stuff," Trevor said, dashing salt and pepper haphazardly over his plate.

"Me too," Cameron said. "The whole concept of this ride concerns me."

Cameron's mom cleared her throat. "Which reminds me, we're going to need some strong cleaner and some more towels after you wrote all over the walls."

"Well, I ran out of window." Cameron scooped up a

glob of syrup-soaked French toast and crammed it in his mouth.

Devin scrunched his nose. "What does that even mean?"

"It means I had to do some calculations in order to soothe my mind," Cameron said. "I get that way whenever something deeply troubles me, or when I forget my pills. Once, on a family campout in Yellowstone, my pills fell into a lake." He twirled his fork. "I then ended up creating a new form of mosquito repellant using deer droppings, kerosene, and mustard."

"And we found him the next morning at another campsite three miles away, wearing only his underwear and covered from head to toe in yellow paste," Ms. Kiffing finished, wearing an unreadable expression. Nika couldn't tell if she was proud or exhausted.

"Yes, but I didn't have a single mosquito bite." Cameron raised his index finger to deliver his point.

"Oh boy," Devin muttered. "Something tells me we're going to love having you with us on the ride."

Cameron beamed at Devin. "Are you all just as worried as I am that this ride will break down?"

"Break down?" Trevor said through a mouthful of eggs. "Why would it do that?"

"This is going to be the first official launch in the Globe," Cameron said. "It's such an enormous entity—the Globe, that is. Plenty of places to be stuck for long periods of time."

Nika wiped her chin with her napkin. Cameron seemed like an odd boy. Did all Americans like to dwell on such dismal topics? She didn't want to think about what terrible things could happen on the Adventure Machine. She just wanted an adventure. A real one, with risks and intrigue. And to experience it without having her grandfather towering over her shoulder and shielding her from danger. "I think we're going to have a wonderful time," she said.

"You speak excellent English," Cameron's mom said, nibbling on a piece of toast. "Did you come to the States to study?"

Nika could sense color forming in her cheeks. "My grandfather had me tutored at home."

"Well, your accent is almost flawless," Ms. Kiffing said. "Would have never guessed you to be from a foreign country."

"Must have cost a pretty penny to pay for that sort of tutoring, eh? Am I right?" Devin's dad asked, winking at Mr. Pushkin.

The older gentleman stared back with an unfriendly gaze and poured cream into his coffee.

"Why didn't you go to regular school?" Devin asked.

"It's just safer for me to be taught at home," Nika said, but then wished she hadn't. She looked down and stared at the table, feeling Devin's and Cameron's gazes take on suspicious gleams.

"Why is it safer?" Trevor asked. "Is the place where you live in Russia dangerous?"

"Perhaps it would be better if we not talk about my granddaughter anymore," Mr. Pushkin said. He took a sip of his coffee and then pushed the cup away.

"Agreed," Cameron said. "I'd rather discuss the dangers of riding the Adventure Machine. I wonder what sort of contingency plans they have in place in case of emergencies?"

"Why do you want to discuss that?" Nika asked.

"I have to think through every possible scenario. It's how I work." Cameron tugged on his collar, and Nika thought the small boy looked just about ready to start undressing.

Cameron's mom slid a small white pill across the table and tapped Cameron's juice with her finger. "My son's truly brilliant, but without his pills, he's hard to swallow. Oh my"— she pressed her hand against her chest and snorted—"that was by no means an intentional pun."

"Mom, please," Cameron hissed.

"If you're so worried about it, why did you even enter the contest?" Devin asked.

Cameron twirled his spoon through the pool of syrup remaining on his plate until it began to froth. "Why do you ask? Is it because I'm younger and smaller than you? Or because of my inexperience on roller coasters?"

"Well, have you ever ridden one before?" Devin asked.

"Literally? No. But in a figurative sense, aren't we all riding this roller coaster called life?" Cameron said with a smile.

Nika laughed. Someone as fragile as Cameron had no business hopping aboard a ride that guaranteed terrifying thrills. Literally or figuratively. But she respected his choice because she felt as though she shared the same path.

Cameron sighed. "I'm here for the science. I find it intriguing how CastleCorp has accomplished creating a ride that will simulate all the things they showcased in their video."

Doug appeared in the food court entrance. At first glance, Nika almost didn't recognize him. Doug had broken character from his usual attire by wearing a dark blue suit and a necktie. He had pulled his floppy blond hair back into a man bun, and instead of sandals, he now wore black shoes. Upon closer examination, Nika noticed they were actually high-top basketball sneakers, but they still seemed fancy for Doug.

"Are we all well fed and rested?" Doug asked as he approached the table, a noticeable chirp in his voice. He squeezed Cameron's shoulders, causing the small boy to yelp in surprise.

"Is it time for us to go?" Cameron asked nervously.

"Almost," Doug said. "We have to wait for my brother. He's escorting Carl Stratton, a high-ranking member of the legal team representing the California Theme Park Approval

Board, to the launch. Thus the suit." He flourished his hand, pointing out his clothing. "This is where it gets a bit hairy."

"How do you mean?" Trevor's mom asked.

Doug shrugged. "Oh, you know, there's little margin for error now. One or two hiccups, and this guy will terminate the whole deal. Life savings down the drain." He whistled and twirled his finger, mimicking the flushing motion of a toilet. "I'm only kidding. Carl Stratton's an old friend and an avid roller coaster aficionado."

Two more people entered the food court. Terry Castleton wore a light brown suit and carried a tablet, which he tapped on using a long silver stylus as he approached. The other was a man with black hair, heavily slicked back with mousse; pale, sallow skin; and thin, smirky lips. The man glanced at everyone at the table, his eyes skimming each of the children with little interest.

"Everyone, this is my brother, Terry," Doug announced. "Hopefully, you recognize him from the video. He hasn't gained too much weight since we shot it."

Terry forced a smile at his brother and then shook everyone's hands. "I apologize for not being present for the initial introductions."

"And this is . . . Who's this?" Doug asked, referring to the other man walking behind Terry. "Is Carl not coming?"

"Mr. Stratton is having his gallbladder removed," Terry

said. "So, no, he won't be coming. This is Mr. Crones from the approval board."

"I take it you're representing the board on Carl's behalf?" Doug asked the greasy-haired man.

"That's right." Mr. Crones reached up to wipe the corner of his eye, and in doing so, he revealed a sparkling, bejeweled bracelet that slipped down from beneath his sleeve. Nika marveled at the unusual piece of jewelry. Were those diamonds?

Doug grinned halfheartedly but turned once more to Terry. "Stratton's been here throughout the project. I wish I'd known sooner."

"Don't we all?" Terry replied. "But gallbladder attacks rarely give sufficient warnings. Should we postpone the launch?"

Doug appeared to consider the offer, but only for a moment. "Of course not. We can't postpone."

"Are you sure? Because I'd be happy to do whatever you wish."

Doug narrowed his eyes at his brother. "We don't have the luxury of postponing, Terry."

"Don't worry, Mr. Castleton," Mr. Crones said. "I understand the situation perfectly, and I can't wait to watch the launch."

*   *   *

The Castletons walked briskly through the halls of the facility with the chain of kids and parents trailing them like an odd family of ducks. Terry spoke to Mr. Crones at the front of the line, but his voice was too low for Nika to hear what they were talking about. Whatever it was, Mr. Crones seemed to find it quite humorous. He snickered and nodded and smoothed his hair against the side of his head with his palm.

"We should all be able to squeeze in," Doug said, once they arrived at the elevator.

There was a murmuring among the group as they each tried to find an open section of floor in the tight space. Nika's grandfather pulled her toward the back corner and acted as a shield between her and the others.

"Everyone comfy?" Doug asked, before inserting a key into the elevator panel, revealing another row of hidden buttons. He pressed the bottom one, and the elevator began to descend.

The elevator dinged as the cart came to a stop. When the door opened, a tall woman wearing a bloody apron appeared in the entrance. The nightmarish figure had pale, gaunt features; sunken eyes; and lips that hung in a permanent snarl. Her hair stood on end, a ratted mess clotted with more of the blood that had been splattered across her apron. She gripped a menacing meat cleaver in one of her gloved hands, which she jabbed at the crowded elevator.

"Hello, maggots," the woman said in a deep, throaty

voice. "I hope you've brought your bibs. Because it's about to get messy!" She then released a bloodcurdling cackle.

Nika felt her heart leap into her throat. She gripped the back of her grandfather's sleeves and cowered from the imposing woman. Most of the other people in the elevator screamed, none louder than Cameron, though Devin's father was a close second.

"Nice one," Trevor said, chuckling as if unimpressed. "I don't know who you're supposed to be, but you're not fooling anyone with that glob of fake blood."

Devin vigorously clapped his hands.

"What are you clapping for?" Cameron's mom demanded.

"That's Shrill Parker. You know, star of *The Butcher's Bride*," Devin explained. "And that's her famous saying. *Bring your bibs!*"

Doug started to laugh, and the adults in the elevator instantly turned on him. "Now, hold on, folks. Allow me to explain. Shrill Parker's an actress, a pretty famous one at that," he said. "One we believe will connect with our audience and help with the advertisement of the Adventure Machine."

Trevor's mom cleared her throat. "Excuse me, but what does this blood-covered woman have to do with your ride?"

It was a cruel joke, if that was what Doug intended. Nika didn't mind surprises, but she knew her grandfather was so close to ending the whole spectacle for her. She could see his jaw tightening, his eyes fuming with disapproval. What were the Castletons trying to prove?

Doug's forehead glistened with perspiration. "Since the Adventure Machine is intended to be a somewhat scary attraction, our marketing team thought it would be appropriate to have a spokesperson that people would associate with fear. Shrill seemed to be the perfect fit. I apologize, but I guess I didn't expect there to be this much uproar over one of our actresses. Let's just try and forget this ever happened. The Suit-Up Room is at the end of this hallway. If it would make everyone feel better, we can excuse Shrill for the remainder of the morning."

"It would make us feel better," Nika's grandfather agreed.

"Oh, it's okay," Nika piped up from behind him. "If she's just an actress she can stay." The woman was only doing her job, and Nika could see the horror queen's countenance instantly shift from an imposing force to one of embarrassment and shame.

"If she stays, I think we'll take the stairs," said Ms. Kiffing.

Shrill lowered her cleaver to her side, her cheeks flushing a deep shade of pink, which was impressive considering how much pasty makeup she had slathered on her face. "I'm so sorry!" she said. "I'll just take my leave and go clean up. I'm really not a bad person, you know. I just play one on the screen." She sounded quite different when not in character, with an almost nasal voice. Shrill bowed respectfully and then leaned in toward Trevor's mom. "And may I add, I just adore your blouse. It is so lovely."

"Really?" Trevor's mom's eyes lit up with surprise as Shrill moved away from the elevator. "That was nice of her to say."

"Oh my gosh," Devin groaned in disbelief. "Did the Butcher's Bride just compliment your mom's shirt? This is quite possibly the worst day of my life."

CHAPTER 12

TWO DOZEN CIRCULAR blobs of shimmering orange cloth hovered suspended above a row of individual pedestals. Behind each of the pedestals, and connected to the back of the blobs, were vacuum-like contraptions swirling the air. The Suit-Up Room was brightly lit by several panels of lights along the ceiling. The walls were metal with enormous bolts riveted from the ground up. Trevor felt the strong suction against his skin as he approached the Outfit Terminal.

"These are our suits?" Trevor asked, running his fingers against the bubble of cloth. "We're going to look like Oompa-Loompas."

"From *Charlie and the Chocolate Factory*?" Devin asked.

"I love that movie, don't you?" Trevor could remember

sitting in his living room giggling as he watched that one girl turning into a blueberry.

"You mean the book by Roald Dahl?" Cameron asked. "Quite entertaining."

Terry pressed a button on the closest pedestal, and the circular blob floating above it began to rise high in the air. "If I can have our first volunteer," he announced. Trevor shot his hand up well before any of the others. "Very good. What size shirt do you wear?"

Trevor scrunched his eyebrows and stared down at his clothes. "How should I know?"

"He's an adult small," his mom said.

Terry typed the information into a computer next to the pedestal. "Thank you, Ms. Isaacs. And I'll also need his preferred pant and shoe sizes."

While Trevor's mom supplied Terry with the measurements, Doug directed Trevor over to a set of three steps rising up to the pedestal.

"Extend your arms out to your sides like wings," Doug instructed.

As Trevor stuck out his arms, the blob lowered until it completely enveloped him in the fabric. His nostrils filled with the pungent fragrance of rubber balloon and baby powder. Within a few seconds, his head poked up through a hole at the top, while the rest of his body remained within.

"I need you to stand perfectly still." Terry pressed another button on the pedestal.

Trevor held his breath as the vacuum suctioned out the air from inside the blob. The fabric clung to his body from just beneath his chin to the soles of his tennis shoes. Even Trevor's fingers were covered in the orange, stretchy material.

Doug squeezed Trevor's bicep. "Is it a perfect fit?"

Trevor stretched his fingers and picked up each foot, staring at the bottoms. "It's like a superhero outfit." He glanced down and saw Devin, Nika, and Cameron gawking at him in amazement. "But it's a little tight around my armpits." Before he could point out any other awkward areas, Terry made the adjustment on the computer, and a light burst of air flowed in from the vacuum. The suit loosened just enough to make Trevor comfortable.

Trevor rolled his shoulders and gave Terry the thumbs-up. "Now, we're talking. What is this stuff?"

"We call it neotanium. It's a hybrid of neoprene and malleable titanium," Terry explained. "What you're wearing is called the Cerebral Apparatus. Using sensors positioned at key points throughout the suit, the Adventure Machine computer connects the minds of all four participants to create a completely unique scenario each time you ride it."

"So does that mean even you don't know what's going to happen to us?" Cameron asked.

Doug smiled and shook his head. "Not even in the slightest."

"And that's safe how?" Cameron demanded.

"You'll be just fine. This is a ride, remember?" Doug said. "Just enjoy yourself."

When all four of the participants were in uniform, Doug led them to a conveyor belt that emptied into the wall. He picked up what looked like a barcode scanner from a grocery store and pulled the trigger. A bright red laser beam shot out, scanning Trevor's head, and a black helmet with a clear Plexiglas visor appeared on the now-rotating conveyor belt. Like the adjusted suit, the helmet was a perfect fit and cradled Trevor's head in a comfortable cushion.

"Why do we have to wear . . ." Trevor's voice trailed off as static crackled in his ears. A light blipped across his visor, and a series of numbers and words appeared.

"Hello," a robotic voice echoed from inside the helmet. "I will be your Virtual Interactive Companion for the duration of your ride," the voice said. "But you may call me VIC."

"No way!" Trevor howled in excitement. "It's like JARVIS from *Iron Man*!"

With everyone now in complete uniform, Doug and Terry moved the four participants over to the entrance.

"Through this door is what we call the Activation Room, which will be the last stop to allow your suits to come fully online. As you take your seats, you'll be doused from our decompression tubes." Doug glanced back at the row of adults. "It's nothing more than dry-ice fog, just for show." He then turned back to the kids. "Once the procedure is done, the next door will open and you'll be greeted by one of our operators. Her name's Candy, and she will be the one who escorts you onto the train."

"You're not coming with us?" Nika cast a wary look back at her grandfather.

"Unfortunately, no one's allowed into the Launching Room without wearing a specialized neotanium suit."

"Why not?" Cameron asked.

"It's standard procedure," Terry explained. "As of right now, there are only six suits allowed on the platform. Five of them belong to you four and Candy. The sixth has been coded to my signature, should any technical problems arise. We'll be watching from the control room with your guardians. As is the case with any theme park roller coaster, you are to stay in the train at all times. And do not attempt to remove the restraints for any reason, or your suits for that matter," he added. "It's for your safety and we'll be collecting data throughout the launch."

"But don't worry," Doug said, chiming in. "You guys are going to have the time of your lives. Just sit back, enjoy yourselves. Are there any questions before we send you in?"

"How long is this ride going to last?" Devin asked.

Doug curled his lip in thought. "You know, it depends."

"Depends? Ridiculous!" Cameron threw his hands up in frustration. "You should know the exact operating sequence of your equipment. Standard roller coasters can take anywhere from thirty seconds to four or five minutes, tops. How long is it?"

"This isn't a standard roller coaster, Cameron," Doug said patiently. "What you'll be experiencing is unlike any ride ever ridden. Your adventure will take as long as it needs to take."

"But—"

Doug held up a hand, silencing Cameron's outburst. "If it makes you feel better, I don't expect the ride to go longer than thirty minutes."

"Thirty minutes?" Cameron gasped. "That doesn't make me feel better at all."

"Seriously!" Trevor pumped his fist. It was like a dream come true. "Thirty whole minutes? Awesome!"

"Yeah, until you spend a half an hour with vomit in your helmet," Cameron grumbled.

"Hush now, dear," Cameron's mom said, patting him on the helmet. "I'm sure vomit will wash out of that neo . . . whatever it's called. Just keep your clothes on. No one wants to ride a roller coaster with a pasty naked boy."

Cameron flared his nostrils and tugged at his collar.

"You're sure you want to go through with this?" Mr. Pushkin asked, approaching Nika and touching her arm as if to inspect the strange, sleek material. "There's no shame in backing out. We could be on a flight this afternoon."

Nika gazed up at her grandfather. "I will be fine, *Dedushka*."

"She's never been safer, Mr. Pushkin. Of that I can assure you," Doug said.

Nika's grandfather frowned at Doug, his eyes steady and determined. "You had better be right, sir. For your sake."

Trevor's mom walked over and squeezed Trevor in her arms. "Be careful on there, okay? Don't do anything foolish."

"I won't," Trevor said.

"I mean it. I want you to stay strapped in at all times. Follow Mr. Castleton's instructions to the letter. This is not an opportunity to show off or forget where you are."

Trevor shrugged her away. "I got it."

Devin grinned at Trevor. "Your mom really doesn't trust you, huh? You must get into trouble all the time."

"You have no idea," Trevor muttered.

"Well, Son, happy trails," Devin's dad said. "Make me proud and all that." Trevor then noticed Mr. Drobbs lean forward and discreetly slip his cellphone into Devin's hand. "Film everything," he whispered. "And bring it back to me in one piece. You hear?"

Devin didn't look too eager to accept the phone, but he nodded tersely and concealed it behind his back. Trevor was actually impressed. Sneaking a recording device onto the secretive launch was a bold move. Would the Castletons actually allow it?

"Okay. You've all said your goodbyes, and you feel good, correct?" Doug asked, taking no notice of Devin's piece of contraband. Doug beamed and flourished his hand behind him. "Right this way, my friends. '"Will you walk into my parlor?" said the spider to the fly.' "

"That statement seems a tad inappropriate, don't you think?" Cameron asked, looking longingly back toward his mom. Ms. Kiffing merely smiled; then the four participants stepped through the door together.

CHAPTER 13

MULTIPLE ROWS OF light beige chairs lined the Activation Room. It resembled the waiting area of an airline terminal, with every four seats broken up into separate sections.

"I wonder why there are so many seats in here?" Cameron said, filing in behind the others. He squished next to Trevor, eyeing the rows of oddly shaped chairs inquisitively.

"You're hugging me, you know that, right?" Trevor asked, glancing down at Cameron.

"Not hugging. Cinching." Cameron moved back an inch. "I'm just making sure we don't get separated."

"Sounds to me like someone's a little nervous," Devin said from the rear. "Having second thoughts? There's the exit if you want to back out."

"Leave him alone," Nika said. Cameron felt her hand press softly against his shoulder. "You're not having second thoughts, are you?"

"No!" Cameron spat. "Not exactly." That was such a ridiculous statement. *Second thoughts.* It implied Cameron lacked the confidence in his own ability to rationally think things through the first time.

Cameron weaved his way to the end of the first row and sat down in the seat next to Trevor. The cushion felt spongy and soft, like a memory-foam pillow. A screen above the door displayed the words *Awaiting Decompression* in bright red lights.

Four platinum-colored tubes rose up from the floor in front of the seats. Nika and Devin quickly sat down in line beside Cameron as the tubes, now looking more like metal vines, continued sprouting from the ground. When the tubes reached their maximum length, the screen above the door changed colors. Instead of bright red, the lights glowed yellow, and the words changed to read *Now Decompressing.*

White fog poured out from the nozzle ends of each of the tubes, completely dousing the four children in a blinding cloud as all the lights in the room went out.

"Hey . . ." Cameron heard Devin starting to protest, but then his voice grew muffled and distant. Cameron strained his eyes to see in the darkness as the gushing of the fog drowned out all other sounds in the room. It lasted for no more than a few seconds. Then the door screen illuminated once more, with the words *Decompression Complete* now glowing in green.

The rest of the overhead fluorescent lights flickered as they turned back on and the door to the Adventure Machine opened.

"Right this way, please." A woman now stood in the opening, wearing a similar suit and helmet. She held her hand at her side, directing the four kids into the next room.

Behind the woman, Cameron saw the Adventure Machine.

It was just like in the video. The cart was sleek and slender, but not incredibly long. It had just four seats, two in the front, and two directly behind. Cameron frowned. Why on earth did they build it so small? It wasn't the most optimal riding contraption, he thought. If the Castletons intended to make any money, it seemed obvious they needed to create a bigger vessel. One that could fit dozens of riders at one time.

The train rested on a single tubular track that hummed with bluish bolts of electricity sparking beneath it. The track headed straight into a massive tunnel in the wall, and from where they stood, Cameron couldn't see to the end of it. He glanced over his shoulder and saw a large window near the ceiling, filled with people staring down. In the middle of the group, he could see his mom watching him.

"Candy, that's your name, right?" Trevor asked the lady

walking in front of them. "Why do you have to wear a suit and helmet?"

"For safety of course," Candy said. "We are live and hot, as you can probably tell." She pointed to the snakes of electricity licking at the bottom of the train.

"What will happen if we touch those?" Cameron asked, falling a step behind from the rest of the group.

"Just don't touch them, and we won't have to find out." Candy kept a straight face and gestured to the cart.

"You're joking?" Cameron asked. "Please tell me she's joking." Did Cameron need to list the safety measures the Adventure Machine was violating to them? Because he would.

Nika immediately volunteered for the back, and the woman assisted her into the cart. Nika was careful not to come in contact with any electricity as she stepped up and then lowered herself into her seat. Devin hurried after, before anyone else could volunteer, and sat next to Nika.

"Don't worry, I'll keep you safe," Devin told her, grinning up at Trevor.

"Who's next?" Candy asked.

Trevor waved off Candy's assistance and leapt into the vehicle. He landed in his seat with a loud thud, causing the cart to shudder from his weight.

Nika braced her hands against the side, glaring at Trevor from behind. "Would you please be careful?"

"Come on, Cameron!" Trevor urged, waving him over

94

excitedly as Candy lowered a loose nylon safety strap over his shoulders and instructed him to buckle it into the seat. "What are you waiting for?"

Cameron curiously eyed the visible currents of electricity as he approached the train. One of the bolts coiled and hissed. "Oh, I don't think so." He squeezed his hands, wringing them together like they were wet dish towels. "I just need to think this thing through, scientifically."

Trevor sighed. "Didn't you do that already?"

Cameron shifted his weight to one side. His heart pounded in his chest. What sort of ride required electrical currents coursing through the track? Cameron looked down once more at his uniform. Why was that even necessary? Cameron had memorized every element from the periodic table as well as every mineral and chemical in existence. How did the Castletons come up with something brand-new like neotanium? It just didn't add up.

"I agreed to participate," Cameron said, his voice squeaking. "But I wasn't fully aware of the conditions until I was able to perceive our traveling device."

Up in the observatory room, Doug cleared his throat through a microphone. "What's the holdup?" His voice cascaded down from the speakers in the ceiling.

"I can't see how a live electrical current is safe, and those safety harnesses are too thin. I don't think I want to do this anymore!" Cameron shouted.

Doug covered the microphone with his hand and spoke for a moment with the rest of the group of adults. "It's fine, Cameron," he said, uncovering the microphone. "If you don't feel comfortable riding, no one's going to force you. However, I feel it is necessary to tell you that this will end the contract, and you will not receive your monetary winnings."

Cameron's mom perked up upon hearing this. Cameron watched as she pushed her way to the front of the group and began arguing with Doug. After a minute of tense discussion, she snatched the microphone from him.

"Let's go, dear. You don't have to do this if you don't want to," Ms. Kiffing spoke tersely into the microphone.

Cameron stared at her, his fingers twitching at his side. No monetary winnings? That meant he'd never have enough money to refurbish his laboratory. The microscope he had his eye on had a price tag of well over fifty thousand dollars all by itself. Cameron glanced over his shoulder at the train and then rapidly snapped his head back to the window.

"Oh fine!" he growled, stomping over to the cart and climbing aboard. "Make sure you strap me in good and tight!"

Candy took up her position at a control station, right next to the cart. "Brace yourselves," she said as she pulled a lever on the console. "Your adventure begins now."

The Adventure Machine shot through the tunnel like a rocket, and they were off.

CHAPTER 14

THE SURGING TRAIN roared down the track. Beyond the tunnel, the walls disappeared, opening into a vast room of blackness. As they started to pick up more speed, Nika felt her skin beginning to pinch and tighten, coercing her mouth to open in a strained grimace. The force grew, with each revolution gaining momentum, as a tremendous weight pressed against her chest. She erupted with quick gasping chirps. Devin was making a low groan. Cameron let out the loudest, most annoying sound of all: a high-pitched whistle that seemed to be coming from his nose. Trevor seemed unfazed by the ride's velocity. He leaned forward against his restraints, both hands high above his head as he cheered.

The cart catapulted straight up, screaming as it climbed.

Within seconds, Nika felt they should've burst through the ceiling of the Globe, but still nothing stopped them. She sank into her seat, her back pressing an indentation into the spongy cushion. This was already too much pressure on her body. Even with the protection of the neotanium suit, she knew she couldn't endure much more before terrible things would happen.

"Up to this point, the ride has simply calculated your collected responses to extreme speeds," VIC's voice explained in Nika's helmet. From the looks on everyone else's faces, they were all hearing the same announcement. The pressure on her body released and she felt able to breathe normally.

"Please tell me that's the worst of it." Nika ran her trembling fingers along her collarbone, gasping. If her grandfather had had even an inkling of what was happening on the ride, he would have never agreed to take her to California.

"Keep your arms and legs inside the cart at all times as you encounter your next experience," VIC said.

Lights began to appear overhead, but not ones connected to any sort of fixture. They seemed to be floating fiery balls burning above. Nika realized they were stars, flashing a myriad of colors. Some of the stars twinkled in the distance, the size of small cars, while others passing by were so immense, they blotted out the black blanket of space behind them. She couldn't grasp how anything could be so big, or how the

Castletons had managed to contain such objects within the Globe. Next, they passed planets with rings like Saturn's and orbiting moons. The Adventure Machine increased in speed as they approached an enormous sphere streaking through the sky.

"It's a comet!" Cameron shouted enthusiastically, trying to lean forward in his seat.

As they pulled up right next to the comet, Nika could hear the deafening sizzle and pop of the orb as it pulsated like a sizzling heart. The white-hot flames hissed, licking the side of the cart. Then, to Nika's astonishment, she watched as Trevor reached out and tried to run his hand across the comet's tail.

"Are you mad?" Nika shouted. "It will burn you!" She could feel the sweltering heat emanating from the comet. Any closer, and the ball would disintegrate Trevor's hand.

"Will it?" Trevor asked, pulling back his fingers. "It's not really a comet, you know? It's just a realistic special effect."

Maybe Trevor was right. It couldn't be real, but still, he had no business trying to grab it. "VIC said to keep our arms and legs inside the cart at all times," Nika said.

"They always say that on roller coasters," Trevor said. "That's like the standard rule."

"Well, then why would you not listen to it?" Cameron asked. "Seems like sound advice to me."

"Because he's just trying to show off for Nika," Devin said.

Trevor looked back at Devin and grinned. "I'm not the one who had to sit by her."

"Stop talking. Both of you!" Nika shook her head in disbelief. They were acting like infants. "And don't touch anything!" She jabbed her finger at Trevor.

Suddenly, the comet winked out of existence, and Trevor groaned in disappointment. A powerful suction took hold of the cone of the Adventure Machine, pulling them forward, the safety restraints seeming as though they would snap from the pressure. Nika tried in vain to push back against her seat, but the vacuum kept her body pressed against the restraints, the nylon material digging into her chest.

Nika held her breath, stiffening her arms and legs, and praying that the weight on her body would subside. She couldn't feel pain and therefore had no way of knowing the damage the pressure was causing. "This is crushing me!" she gasped. "It needs to stop!"

"Is that a black hole?" Devin pointed to a swirling mass growing in the distance.

"Oh dear," Cameron gulped. "It would appear so."

"But not a real black hole," Trevor said. "None of this is real."

Lightning bolts zigzagged across the black hole as it hungrily gobbled stars and planets and mountain-sized asteroids into its gaping mouth.

"That is *awesome!*" Trevor threw his hands above his head as the train continued its approach toward the monstrous hole. Then, with a powerful jolt, his body slammed forward against his safety harness. The Adventure Machine screeched to a complete stop, and the black hole immediately disappeared, along with all evidence of space travel. There were no more stars or planets. A misty, paintlike blackness possessing a damp, sulfuric smell gathered around the cart. It wasn't long before Cameron started gagging.

"Eww!" Devin said. "It smells like rotten eggs."

"No, it smells like Yellowstone," Cameron wheezed. "I went there once. . . ."

"Yeah, we know," Trevor said. "You made paste out of mustard and junk."

"That's right. I shared that story already."

The blackness fizzled and dispersed, and Nika's eyes slowly adjusted, and she could see that they were still on the track, the cart balancing on the single tubular line. There was no way to be certain, but it looked as though they had come to a stop somewhere at the center of the massive Globe. Skeletal walls towered above them on every side, and peering over the edge, Nika couldn't see to the bottom.

"Oh no!" Devin shouted from the backseat. "Where is it?"

Nika looked over and saw Devin frantically searching his seat and the floor by his feet.

"Are you sitting on it?" Devin asked Nika. "Will you please move?"

Nika reared back as Devin patted the cushion next to her. "Sitting on what?"

Devin yanked at his safety harness, trying to wiggle free, but the belt remained latched. "This can't be happening!"

"Did you lose your phone?" Trevor asked.

Devin's head shot up and he glared at Trevor, holding out his hand. "How did you know that? You took it didn't you? Give it back or else!"

"I didn't take your dumb phone, Devin," Trevor said. "It probably just fell out when we were shooting through, you know, space and stuff."

"Kind of a risky move, bringing an electronic device onto a ride powered by high-voltage electricity," Cameron said. "The charge alone no doubt destroyed your phone's internal components."

"Shut up, all right?" Devin hissed. "My dad's going to kill me!"

"It was just an accident," Nika said. "He'll understand. He seems very nice."

"You don't know my dad," Devin barked. "I just hope he was able to load some of his video footage to the cloud before he gave it to me. If not, I'm dead."

"How has your adventure been so far?" VIC's voice piped

in through their helmets, and Devin slumped back in his seat, his face red and sweaty.

"We're loving every second of it!" Trevor answered.

Devin folded his arms and huffed. "Speak for yourself."

"I'm a little concerned," Nika said softly. "I didn't know we would be experiencing all that pressure. What if we sustained injuries? VIC, could you scan us to see if we're okay?"

"Certainly," VIC agreed. "Nika, your heart rate is one hundred and sixty beats per minute. Your blood pressure is one thirty-nine over ninety. Your vitals are elevated, to be certain, but nothing to be alarmed about. All initial scans indicate you are in proper health."

Nika caught her breath. It didn't seem possible. She had spent months and months at different hospitals, with doctors and specialists. All of them trying to find ways for her to live a somewhat normal life. Nothing worked. She always had to be so cautious. Nika stared down at the protective layer of neotanium covering her arms.

"What about mine?" Trevor asked.

"Trevor, you have a heart rate of sixty-five beats per minute and a blood pressure of one-twenty over eighty," VIC said.

"Is that bad?" Trevor asked.

"That's normal," Cameron scoffed. "Your vitals aren't elevated at all."

"How are you so relaxed?" Nika asked.

Trevor shrugged. "I feel fine."

Cameron smacked the side of his helmet with his neotanium-gloved hand. "What are my vitals?"

"I'm sorry, Cameron," VIC said. "But I am unable to calculate your heart rate or blood pressure at this time. I'll check back later."

Devin snickered. "It's like you're dead."

Cameron whirled on Devin, his eyes widening. "Don't say that!"

From somewhere above the track arose the mechanized clatter of grinding gears and the soft, muted sound of bells. Nika looked up and saw a circular sphere descending. The sphere resembled a robotic eye, with a bright blue lens connected to a long metal tube that extended down from some unseen location.

"Please hold perfectly still while the Ganglion determines your destiny." This voice came from outside of Nika's helmet. It sounded inhuman and robotic, as though the grinding gears had suddenly discovered how to form words.

"Ganglion?" Trevor asked. "What is that supposed to mean?"

"I think it means command center." Cameron's voice shook noticeably. "A ganglion is like the nervous system. It controls everything within the body."

Nika braced herself for the worst. Would they dive into a landscape overflowing with lava or cruise in blizzard-like conditions? Would a wall of water wash over them, soaking them from head to toe?

Four beams of bluish light shot out from the Ganglion's eye and fell upon each of their helmets. "Computing, computing, computing," the voice repeated over and over for several seconds, echoing throughout the Globe. Nika couldn't be certain, but she thought she noticed a slight tremor travel through the Ganglion's eye and up the long tube.

"Guys?" Devin's voice rose above the annoying "Computing" drone of the Ganglion.

"It has to be finishing soon, don't you think?" Nika asked. The scan had gone on for more than a minute, and now she was positive she could see the tube above the eye beginning to shake.

"Guys?" Devin forcibly repeated. "We need to stop this."

Nika glanced over at him.

In his hands, he held a small black device, with his thumb hovering above a white button.

Trevor pressed against his seat restraints to more fully face Devin. "What are you holding?"

"It says *abort*," Devin said, showing the others the word above the button. "It's under each of our seats."

Nika looked at her feet and noticed the corner of a similar device resting on the floor of the cart. "It's probably just for emergencies, right?"

"Right," Cameron agreed. "Most likely a way to stop the

ride if things should go awry. It would make sense to include such a method."

"Why do you look so pale?" Nika asked, staring at Devin suspiciously. "Are you not feeling well?"

Devin looked at each of them, sweat trickling down his forehead, his eyes taking on a look of panic. Then he turned his attention to the remote in his hands and, without a word of explanation, he pressed his thumb down on the button.

CHAPTER 15

DEVIN STARED AT the button. He heard it click beneath his thumb and he waited for something to happen. The lights would come on and that weird Ganglion thing would shut down and stop chanting overhead. The ride needed to end. That much he knew, though he had no idea why.

"What are you doing?" Trevor exclaimed, reaching back and trying to swat the remote out of Devin's hands.

Devin held on, refusing to drop it. "It's not working," he said desperately.

Cameron looked terrified as he spun around to face Devin. "I don't think you should be tampering with the equipment. The ramifications could be severe."

Above them, the Ganglion continued its droning mantra. "Computing, computing, computing."

Devin's eyes lit up. "Maybe we all have to push it to stop the ride."

"But we're not done yet." Trevor waved his hand behind him, gesturing to the black, open space. "Is this because you lost your dad's phone?"

"No!" Devin snapped. "This has nothing to do with it." At least, he didn't think it did. His premonitions didn't always have specific reasons. True, his dad was going to throw a fit when he discovered that Devin had lost his phone, but there was something else causing the tingling sensation in Devin's chest. A warning of something bad that was about to happen. But unlike in other instances, he couldn't see exactly what it was. Just that he knew they needed to be off the Adventure Machine.

"So stop messing around and push the button." Devin nodded to the others, instructing them to follow his lead.

Trevor laughed. "No one else wants to stop the ride. Just you."

From the front seat arose another click, and Trevor spun around as Cameron depressed his button with both thumbs.

"Wait!" Trevor shouted.

"If he thinks we should stop, there's probably a great reason for it," Cameron said, cowering away.

Devin stared directly at Trevor. "I have a really bad feeling right now."

Cameron shivered. "A bad feeling? Like the kind you . . . you know, normally get?"

"Shut up, goob!" Devin hissed, and Cameron immediately clamped his mouth closed.

"What are you talking about?" Trevor demanded. "What's he talking about?"

"Nothing." Devin flashed Cameron a warning glance. No one was supposed to know about his ability, and yet, somehow, the little brainiac had discovered Devin's secret. If Cameron clued the others in on it, they would never let Devin live it down. Just like everyone else in Devin's school once they found out. He could already hear their name-calling. Psycho Devin Drobbs and his mystic crystal ball.

Nika looked apologetically at Trevor and then bent over to pick up her remote. "We could restart after we get back to the station, right?" she asked, just before pressing her finger on the button.

Trevor dug his hands against the sides of his helmet. "They're all watching us right now. Think about that," Trevor said. "Doug and Terry, our parents. The whole world! I don't think they'll be super excited about us backing out, and we won't get paid."

From overhead, the Ganglion suddenly released a loud,

echoing chime, and the blue beams of light flashing upon the four helmets vanished.

"Scanning complete." The sphere began to ascend into the darkness.

In front of the cart, less than twenty yards down the track, a large circle appeared. Disklike and composed of more of the bluish light, the circle began to spin. Devin was about to ask the others what they thought was the point of the giant glowing Frisbee, when he noticed a dramatic change occurring to the circle. Instead of spinning, swirling lights, it was suddenly a window showing lush green trees and a hazy purple sky behind it. The disk expanded until it was large enough for them to move through.

As the cart continued approaching the hole, the jungle landscape formed more fully into view. Devin could not only see the canopy of trees and vines, but also the distinct cone shape of an erupting volcano towering in the midst of it. Black smoke billowed from the top, blotting out the sky. A burst of intense humidity wafted over the group, and Devin could smell the horrendous stench of something rotten, like raw sewage, permeating his nostrils. It smelled as if an animal had died somewhere just beyond the hole.

"I'm pretty sure this place is prehistoric, don't you think?" Trevor asked, glancing over his shoulder.

"Yeah, maybe," Nika said.

"We still have time to abort the ride," Devin insisted, his brow furrowed.

Trevor grinned. "We're not stopping until I see what's making that awful smell. Five bucks says it's the rotting carcass of a brontosaurus."

As the nose of the cart passed through the circle, dipping as it entered, Devin leaned forward, craning his neck, until he could see the track descending through a wall of green-and-brown foliage. In front of him, Cameron, as if in a trance, repeatedly pressed his abort button.

Down they swooped into the thick vegetation, leaves and branches scratching against Devin's suit. The hill wasn't as steep as he'd initially thought, and soon the cart leveled off, the trees thinning into a clearing where a roaring river flowed just off to the side of the track. He could smell the clear, fresh scent of water as condensation formed on the outside of his visor. The sky overhead had changed from purple into a dark black from the roiling volcanic fumes.

"How's this even possible?" Nika's voice rang out, muted by the river.

"It's awesome!" Trevor shouted. "This is what I signed up for. A real adventure. Something we'll never forget."

"What is that?" Cameron urgently pointed to the other side of the river. A large catlike creature crouched within a patch of taller grass, watching the cart, its long tail whipping behind it. Devin could see tusks jutting out from its gaping mouth.

Cameron gulped. "I do believe that's a saber-toothed tiger."

"It's not real," Nika said. "It can't be."

"Looks pretty real to me," said Devin. "And I bet it spears things with those tusks. Like kids on roller coasters." His voice turned high-pitched, as the saber-toothed cat leapt over the river and landed a few yards from the track. The creature cocked its head to one side in curiosity as the train began to roll once more.

"It's going to chase us," Trevor said. "I guarantee it's going to chase us." He leaned over the edge, smacking the side of the cart to get the animal's attention. "Come and get us!"

"Are you out of your mind?" Devin screamed. Why was Trevor acting that way? In the beginning, Devin just assumed Trevor was constantly trying to impress the others. But now he wasn't so sure. It seemed as though Trevor genuinely wanted the creature to chase them.

Two more cats, with equally enormous tusks, emerged from the jungle, dashing toward them. The train started moving faster, picking up speed, but the snarling creatures kept pace for several hundred yards, their clawed feet whipping mud in their wake. Nika leaned farther into the cart, trying to put extra distance between her and the animals as one of them raked its claws along the metal cart. Despite their determination and their powerful legs propelling them forward, the cats were no match for the intense speed of the Adventure Machine. Within a few moments, Devin watched the creatures shrink in the distance until they were two reddish specks on the horizon.

"Bummer," Trevor said. "We didn't even get a chance to see one up close."

"That was close enough," Nika said. "Where did they find such creatures?"

Something heavy thudded against the cart. Devin snapped his head back just in time to see a rock, easily the size of a laundry basket, bounce off the hood. Another rock followed, barely missing the cart. Devin could feel the rushing wind as it passed.

"It's a meteor shower!" Cameron pointed to the sky. "We're going to get crushed!"

The Adventure Machine continued racing through an expansive green meadow brimming with squat, leafy bushes. The jungle was nothing more than a blurry outline behind them, and overhead the sky continued to bombard the earth with debris. Doug Castleton had said they were using advanced technology, but the kids had never expected this. When their seats suddenly began to vibrate and the cart wobbled uneasily on the track, they braced themselves for what they thought would be an earthquake. But then there was the sound of the engine winding down beneath the hood, as the four safety harnesses securing the kids in their seats unlatched.

"Please exit the cart in an orderly fashion," VIC's voice announced through their helmets.

"What do you mean, 'exit the cart'?" Devin demanded. "Weren't you the one who told us earlier to stay in the cart at all times?" And now the disembodied voice had flip-flopped. They were headed for disaster. It was only a matter of time. No. They needed to stay right where they were and wait for this part of the ride to end.

Cameron tried cramming the metal hook of his seat belt back into its buckle, but it refused to latch. Two more meteors, twice as big as the first ones, rammed the earth, sending out a powerful shockwave. Devin could feel his chest vibrate from the immense force and the heat radiating from the sizzling boulder just a few yards from where they sat.

"Front riders should exit first," VIC continued, "from left to right, followed by the rear riders. Please, do so now."

"We'll be flattened," Nika said, gripping her safety harness. "Why are you making us leave?"

They waited for a response, but VIC gave none.

Trevor slipped the harness straps from his shoulders and stood up. "I guess we get out." He looked at the others. "Let's get going."

Cameron eyeballed Trevor as though he were covered in

ants. "I can't see how hiking through this wilderness makes any feasible sense. And let us not forget about the meteors."

Trevor searched the sky for more of the falling rocks. "That's the last of them, I think."

Fffffooom!

Another huge meteor, the size of a truck, thudded several yards away, shaking the ground beneath them. Cameron leapt down from his seat and clung to Trevor's arm.

"I actually did see that one, but I didn't think it would land that close. My mistake," Trevor said.

Cameron tested his weight on each foot. "It's solid ground. This bush"—he plucked an elephant-ear-like leaf from a nearby plant—"it must be plastic, or made of some sort of synthetic material." Cameron ripped the leaf into two pieces, and bright yellow ooze dripped from the tear. "That smells awful. And it feels real!"

"Where are we supposed to go?" Devin asked, still rooted to his seat. "It's just a wide-open space."

"You will now proceed on foot," VIC answered. "I will continue to assist you for the remainder of your ride."

Nika slowly rose, but when Trevor offered his hand to help, she shook her head. "No, thank you. I'll do this myself," she said as she climbed over the edge of the cart.

"This is just plain stupid." But Devin reluctantly got out. "What kind of ride makes you walk?"

"Excellent," VIC said once the four of them had exited the vehicle. "Please, watch your toes."

"Watch our what?" Devin glanced down at his feet just as the Adventure Machine suddenly roared back to life. Before any of them could try to climb back into their seats, the cart erupted down the track, pelting them with clumps of grass and mud, and abandoning them in the middle of the meadow.

CHAPTER 16

IT MADE NO sense to Cameron to go chasing after the accelerating Adventure Machine. He had never been particularly fast. Running really wasn't his thing. And if the two jungle cats couldn't catch the cart, the kids didn't stand a chance.

"Now what do we do, genius?" Devin asked, glaring at Trevor.

Trevor blinked. "Are you calling me a genius?"

"You're the one who told us to get out of the cart."

"Technically, VIC instructed us to leave the safety of the vehicle," Cameron corrected. "Trevor was just following orders. Also, technically, *I'm* the genius."

"Yeah, whatever," Devin said. "A lot of good it did us. Now we're stranded."

"You're just mad because you lost your dad's phone," Trevor said. "Accidents happen, dude. Let it go."

"Let's not argue," Nika said. "It's called the Adventure Machine, and this *is* an adventure, right?"

"Please head due south toward the waterfall," VIC's voice chimed in.

Trevor glanced at Cameron. "Which way's south?"

Cameron's head perked up. It's not like he had a compass, and his helmet's GPS function, if it had one, which Cameron assumed it did, wasn't functioning at the moment. Pinpointing their precise location would present a unique challenge.

"Well, it's not clear," Cameron said. "If we could use standard star constellations, we'd have a much easier time in determining a point of reference. These stars look unfamiliar to me. I wonder if our visors could solve this quandary. VIC, could you display our coordinates on my screen?"

"Or you could just look with your eyes." Nika pointed to a spot behind them where a solitary mountain rose up, no more than half a mile away. An enormous waterfall gushed from an opening midway up the mountain's peak, cascading down like a sparkling ribbon.

"Okay, there's no way I didn't see that before," Devin said.

Cameron folded his arms and shifted his weight to one side. *Odd.* Where had that mountain come from? The Adventure Machine must be using mirrors. Or was it possible that the Castletons managed to drape something over the landscape? He suddenly snapped his fingers.

"Of course! It's simply an impressive three-dimensional display," Cameron said. "Which explains how they can so readily manipulate the environment. I'm actually embarrassed it took me this long to understand."

Trevor reached over and squeezed Cameron's shoulder. "You're not making sense."

Cameron swallowed. "It's just an elaborate projection. It's like we're in a movie, only instead of it being flashed in front of us on a screen, we're actually in a screen that's all around us, and therefore makes it appear as though we've gone somewhere else."

"Like space or ten trillion BC to prehistoric times," Devin said.

Cameron's head bobbled. "Yes, but ten trillion BC is a bit much for prehistoric. And if we're going to be technical, judging by those saber-toothed cats, that was most likely the Eocene period."

"I was trying to agree with you," Devin said.

"Oh, well, thank you." Cameron smiled. "But if you're going to agree with me, it doesn't hurt to be accurate."

Nika shook her head. "But the heat and the smells. How are they making it so real?"

"Olfactory emissions," Cameron answered, his head

flitting back and forth between Nika, Devin, and Trevor. Judging by their baffled expressions, Cameron had to assume they had never heard the term before. He sighed. Was he supposed to dumb everything down to their level? "There are probably hundreds, if not thousands, of scent dispensers throughout the Globe. And do you really think increasing the temperature is that difficult? It's just a flip of a switch. Don't you see? Logic solves all. Honestly, I'm embarrassed I fell for such an obvious ruse. It just feels so real."

Nika bent over and caressed the long, flappy leaf of one of the nearby plants. "Does your logic explain this?"

Cameron flipped his hand dismissively. "True, that does look and feel like an actual plant. Maybe the Castletons are just good gardeners."

The ride was nothing more than a trick. An optical illusion. A way to fool one's brain into believing you had done the impossible and crossed into another world. Cameron couldn't help but feel impressed by the Castletons' brilliance. With that sort of liberty, they could conjure up any number of scenarios to project within the Globe. All they needed were willing participants and control of the thermostat.

Devin stared at the mountain towering a short distance away. "So what are we supposed to do once we reach that waterfall?"

"We just need to listen to VIC," Nika said. "He will instruct us on where we should go."

Cameron cringed when, instead of VIC's voice, loud static filled his helmet. The distortion lasted for a few seconds and then fell silent.

"Quit playing around, VIC," Devin growled. "Tell us what to do."

Only silence followed, not even the crackle of static. And then Cameron noticed something unusual appear in the upper left-hand corner of his visor.

OFF-LINE

"Are all your visors off-line?" Cameron asked.

Each of the others nodded.

Nika lightly tapped the side of her helmet. "Do you think we broke something?"

"Maybe you guys did when you all pressed your abort buttons," Trevor said, a slight smile cracking across his lips.

Nika looked at Cameron, her eyes widening. "Could that be true?"

Cameron puffed his cheeks. "How could I possibly know that? I say we head for the waterfall, and maybe VIC will come back online to tell us where to go next."

Trevor patted Cameron on the back. "Of all the things you've said today, that one makes the most sense."

CHAPTER 17

FROM A LOGICAL standpoint, Cameron had yet to determine
if the Adventure Machine was indeed providing a fun-filled
experience. He had never been one to enjoy a whooshing plunge or the sensation of being flipped upside down
over and over until his toes throbbed. On the other hand,
the science of the Adventure Machine fascinated him. The
simulated journey into space and the subsequent landing in
a primitive destination with flourishing wildlife and actual
strong-smelling vegetation was indeed a marvel.

"Are you all right back there?" Nika called out to Cameron.

"Yes, yes, I'm fine. I'm just thinking," he replied.

"Well, maybe you should try to keep pace with the rest of
us," she suggested.

Cameron glanced up from staring at the thick, spongy grass squishing beneath his feet and noticed that several yards had spread out between him and the others. The mountain with the waterfall had proven to be quite a distance away, and the group had been walking for almost ten minutes.

"Maybe you should consider walking slower," Cameron grumbled to himself, picking up his pace.

Cameron stared at the back of Devin's helmet as he walked at the head of the group. When Cameron had found out that Devin would be joining them on the Adventure Machine, he was overwhelmed with excitement. Most people as gifted as Cameron knew about Devin's ability. You didn't have to dig deep on the Internet to find articles about the peculiar boy. He wasn't a psychic, because that, of course, was ridiculous, but Devin definitely had the ability to sense certain events before they took place. Which made what had happened earlier on the ride all the more troubling. Why did Devin have the sudden urge to end the ride less than a few minutes after the launch? Did he foresee a tragedy?

And then there was Trevor, who seemed like a nice enough boy, but he was born completely fearless. Only a handful of people in the world had a misfiring amygdala. Cameron tried to make sense of it all. What were the odds of bumping into not one but two scientific anomalies on the same ride? And then, if you threw in Cameron, who was considered by *Whiz Kid Weekly* to be one of the most brilliant child geniuses on the planet, the plot grew thicker still. Cameron found himself grinning widely as he remembered the article about himself in the magazine. It included a really good picture that went with it.

"Focus!" Cameron whispered to himself.

The only participant who broke Cameron's theory was Nika. He knew hardly anything about her, other than her grandfather's occupation. Gazing in Nika's direction, Cameron's eyes narrowed. She was definitely keeping something from them. She had to be. And if she was, then that meant . . . What? What did that mean?

He suddenly felt the urge to solve something. Where was his whiteboard or a large pane of glass and a marker when he needed them? Oh, and a can or two of Kraken Spit. Cameron's suit had taken on a cramped sort of feel to it. He tugged at his collar and pulled at his sleeves, but the neotanium material clung to him like plastic wrap covering his mom's burned pumpernickel bread. What he wouldn't give for some privacy to solve a few things in his underwear.

Something small, brown, and furry scuttled past Cameron's foot. He leapt back in surprise, but kept control of his urge to scream out.

"Wait up for a second," he yelled to the others. Nika stopped and so did Trevor. Devin scowled back at Cameron and then mumbled something to Trevor before throwing his hands up in frustration to wait with the others.

"I found something," Cameron said. "It's some sort of creature." He squinted, stooping down to one knee, as the tiny animal tried to hide beneath the folds of a leafy bush. Cameron's fingers trembled as he parted the leaves to inspect his finding. The creature hissed angrily, and Cameron gasped, toppling back on his behind.

Trevor hurried over and steadied Cameron with his hand. "What is it?"

Cameron swallowed. "That's odd."

"What's odd?" Devin asked skeptically.

Cameron pointed to the plant, his eyes widening behind his glasses. The Castletons were playing a cruel, cruel game. Of all the things they could've selected for the Adventure Machine, why did they have to choose this specific creature? He furrowed his brow in thought, trying to determine how Doug or Terry would've discovered his secret fear. As far as he knew, it wasn't recorded in any of his databases. Not even his mom knew about it. "Either this is a spectacular coincidence, or the Castletons know way more about us than we think."

"Why do you have to talk like that?" Trevor asked. "If you just spoke like a normal person, maybe we could help you."

"This is the only way I know how to talk!" Cameron shouted. "I was born this way. Brilliant. Misunderstood. Do you want me to put it in terms you can understand? Should I speak like a caveman in grunts and growls?" He once again pointed anxiously at the bush, his heart throbbing in his chest. "Would someone please see if it's gone?"

Nika carefully bent down and peeled back one of the leaves. She stared for a moment, her eyes inquisitive before they softened. "Aw, it's so sweet." When she removed her hand from under the bush, Nika held an animal no bigger than a rodent.

Trevor and Devin leaned forward for a closer look, while Cameron tried to squirm away.

"Is it a moose?" Devin asked.

Nika nodded. "I believe it is. I've never seen one so small."

The creature had a set of antlers and four knobby legs, and it blinked up at Nika through a pair of pinprick eyes.

"That's what you're afraid of?" Trevor reached out his hand, and Nika gently passed the creature into his palm. "It's as big as a hamster."

"I don't care how big it is. It's a moose, okay? I don't like them. I never have." Cameron scrambled to his feet, sticking his tongue out in disgust as Trevor began petting the creature's antlered skull.

"Hate to break it to you," Devin said. "But it looks like there's more of them." He pointed to a quivering patch of leaves a few feet away.

Dozens of miniature moose darted out from beneath the bulbous plant, like a burrow of cockroaches fleeing from the light. The moose produced a high-pitched *squee* as they ran, kicking up thin furrows of dust behind them.

"Look at them all!" Nika clasped her hands together. "There are dozens of them."

"Yeah, just in that bush." Trevor nodded to another cluster of shrubs, leaves quaking from the ongoing activity of scurrying moose beneath them.

"So, that's kind of freaky," Devin said.

Cameron groaned, a fit of nausea threatening to overtake him. Judging by how the unusual plants appeared to harbor the disgusting little creatures, and calculating the sheer volume of vegetation dotting the landscape, Cameron estimated there could be at least ten thousand pocket-sized moose out there, waiting to strike.

"We need to go," Cameron said, his voice squeaking.

"Yes, I agree." Nika backed away from the bush, nudging up against Cameron's arm. "Why do you think they're here?"

Wanting to put as much distance as possible between himself and the army of creatures, Cameron turned to run. "The Castletons have somehow found out about my deepest fear and inserted it into . . ." He couldn't finish the sentence.

A colossal moose stood less than twenty yards away, noisily chomping a mouthful of leaves. Feathery strands of cobwebs dangled from its antlers, which were so big that they were more like mangled billboards.

Cameron spun around to face the others. He blinked rapidly and started hyperventilating. This was why he never went camping anymore. Well, this and the mustard incident.

Trevor laughed, gawking at the gigantic creature. "No way! That must be their mother. Do moose even get that big?"

Nika held her finger up to her lips and crouched down on her knees. "Stay quiet. Keep low so we don't seem like a threat to it."

Devin didn't argue as he ducked down beside her. Nika urgently motioned to Trevor, who joined them on his knees.

Cameron dropped to the ground and curled himself up into a ball. "Not the mother, it's not the mother," he muttered. "It's clearly a male, you idiots." Was he the only one who understood zoology?

"Cameron's not in a good place right now." Trevor cupped his hands over his mouth to project his voice, while maintaining a whisper. "Probably not the best idea to lie down right in its path."

"I'm playing dead! Doesn't anyone read? If I play dead, it'll bypass me and charge after someone else." Where were his pills when he needed them? The inside of Cameron's suit felt like boiling rubber. It clung to him, itchy and constrictive. He rolled to one side and peered up at the monstrosity looming almost cartoonlike above him, blotting out a surprisingly expansive chunk of the horizon. Cameron's mind began to whir like a computer processor. The leafy vegetation scattered in clusters all around them stood no more than a foot off the ground. Using the plants as a starting point, he calculated the moose's height. From the bottom of its hooves to the top of its massive skull, the animal towered at least twenty-four and a half feet above the ground.

Cameron suddenly uncurled his legs and hopped up onto his feet. "Impossible! You're not real!" He pointed vigorously at the moose. Twenty-four feet? No quadrupedal creature in the animal kingdom reached such heights. Even the world's tallest giraffe stood a foot or two shorter than that. "This is just one of your tricks, isn't it, Doug? A clever scheme to ignite fear within us? Well, ha!" Cameron marched all the way up to the moose. When he stood beneath it, his helmet failed to reach the bottom of one of its lanky kneecaps.

"Great," Devin moaned. "Now we're going to have to carry his corpse the rest of the way."

"Yeah, what are you doing, Cameron?" Trevor shouted.

Cameron jabbed his finger above him. "I'm proving a point. This is not an actual living entity. It's a projection. Just like I said earlier. We're seeing things through these helmets." Of course! Cameron didn't actually realize the truth of it all until he spoke it out loud. The suits and the helmets were the final pieces of the mysterious Adventure Machine puzzle. In order for the ride to truly function, you needed a vehicle, elaborate projections to showcase the images, and then a screen to view them on. The visors acted as those screens. "I believe I've graduated into a whole new level of genius!"

The moose stopped chomping on the leaves and lowered its head in Cameron's direction. Black, lidless eyes, like a pair of softballs, stared at him. It bristled, the thick tuft of hair on its neck standing on end. Then the moose bent down, nostrils flaring, as it curiously sniffed Cameron.

Cameron tried to laugh, but when the moose's muzzle pressed against his helmet, knocking him off balance and gumming up his visor with a sort of opalescent mucus, it was a miracle he kept his breakfast down.

"Wait. How did you just knock me down?" Cameron gulped. "You're just a big, real moose. *El gigante!*" And then he fainted into a tiny heap on the ground.

CHAPTER 18

MOOSE DON'T EAT people, do they? Trevor wondered as he watched the giant creature stoop over Cameron, dragging its tongue across the tiny boy's helmet.

Nika clung to Trevor's arm, yanking on his sleeve. "How do we help him?" Her voice was high-pitched and panicked. Devin was speechless, his fists clenched at his sides, unable to move.

"Hold on."

Trevor trotted toward the large animal and the bundle of Cameron lying lifeless at its feet. Trevor puffed out his chest and flailed his arms above his head, shrieking as he ran. He just needed to establish dominance. Most creatures dwelling in their natural habitat respected a dominant human. Trevor remembered that from a documentary on gorillas he had watched a few months ago.

As Trevor approached, the moose recoiled in surprise. A clump of mushy, chewed-up vegetation dropped from its mouth. It snarled, jerking its head from side to side, before lunging at Trevor. One of the antlers barely missed him as Trevor somersaulted out of the way.

"Well, that didn't work," he said, catching his breath. Maybe moose were the exception to the rule in the animal kingdom.

He scrambled to his feet as the creature attacked again, its antlers swinging wide, once again missing their mark. Then, the moose bent down once more and opened its mouth as if to swallow Cameron whole.

Trevor rolled his eyes. "You're going to eat him?" he asked. "You have an entire world of grass all around you, and you're going to eat Cameron?"

The moose's eyes suddenly glowed red, its mouth widening.

Trevor laughed. "Red eyes? Seriously? How cheesy is that?" For Trevor, the red eyes solidified to him that the moose couldn't be real. And since the creature had managed to touch Cameron, it wasn't a virtual creation of some projector either. Which meant it was a robot, or something else Trevor couldn't explain. Either way, he didn't really believe the Castletons would allow the moose to carry through with its plan to eat Cameron. And yet, something told Trevor he shouldn't just sit there and not respond. Even if he had brought it on himself, Cameron needed help.

"How do I knock that thing down?" Trevor asked.

Something whizzed overhead, and Trevor glanced up in time to see a small rock strike the creature on its snout. The moose clamped its mouth shut in surprise and released an agitated hiss. Trevor's head swiveled as another projectile shot through the air, ricocheting off the moose's antlers. Nika and Devin had gathered armfuls of rocks and they took turns throwing them at the target.

"Great shot!" Trevor cheered, after yet another rock struck the moose's shoulder.

"Just get Cameron!" Nika shouted.

The annoyed animal reared back on its hind legs, pawing at the barrage of rocks. Trevor raced in and ducked beneath its hooves. He grabbed Cameron beneath his armpits and pulled him out of the way. Behind Trevor arose the piercing cry of what sounded like a million angry mosquitoes. Then the ground began to patter. It wasn't an earthquake, or even loud enough to be confused with thunder, but a wave of the miniature moose charging out from their hiding places. They squealed, racing directly toward Trevor and Cameron, but then moved wide, arcing out to avoid the two boys, before climbing up the gigantic moose's legs.

Nika threw one more rock, which hit the creature squarely on its chest. It howled and shuddered and then turned to retreat.

Trevor reached down and shook Cameron by his shoulder. "Hey, wake up, sleepyhead. No time for naps now." He had seen people faint in movies all the time, but it had always looked fake. But not Cameron. The small boy had collapsed like an action figure, arms and legs folded in on each other.

"Is he really still asleep?" Devin asked. "After all that?"

Trevor shrugged. "I guess so." He drummed his fingers on Cameron's visor.

Cameron swatted at Trevor's hand, grumbled something incoherent, and peeled his eyes open, one at a time.

"Can you move, or are you hurt?" Nika asked, squatting down beside Trevor and snapping her fingers softly next to Cameron's helmet.

"I'm fine," Cameron grumbled. "I just had a hyper overload. It happens." He tensed, his small hands clenching into fists as he looked desperately up at Trevor. "Is it gone?"

Trevor sucked back on his teeth. "Not exactly, but you shouldn't look."

Cameron didn't listen, turning to search for the moose. When he found it, he produced a sound similar to that of a smoke alarm's warning chirp.

"I told you not to look," Trevor said.

The creature had moved a decent distance away from the group, to where it no longer felt threatening, but the throngs of baby moose had gathered in a cluster on the giant's back. To Trevor, it kind of looked like a mutated wolf spider, toting about its miniature offspring.

"What happened after I passed out?" Cameron asked, watching the moose suddenly bristle and then gallop across the meadow with long, awkward strides.

"Uh . . ." Trevor glanced at Nika. She discreetly shook her head and whispered to Trevor not to tell Cameron the truth. Trevor agreed. If Cameron discovered how the moose had almost swallowed him, he'd never be the same.

"What's that on its back?" Cameron demanded, turning back to face them.

"The babies," Devin said. "They all freaked out and climbed aboard their momma."

"Daddy," Cameron replied meekly. "It's their daddy. You can tell by the antlers."

"Are you sure?" Devin asked.

Cameron started to nod, but then that petered away. "No, I'm not so sure about anything anymore. I don't understand how I could physically feel the moose. It had definite substance. No virtual projection could simulate such authenticity."

"Maybe it's a robot," Trevor suggested.

"A robot?" Cameron scoffed. His lip curled in thought and then he shrugged. "I suppose that's a feasible option. The Castletons sure went to great lengths to create something so uniquely frightening as a robotic moose."

"Why are you so scared of moose?" Trevor asked. All of Trevor's past friends were scared of something. Snakes. Bees. Monkeys. But this was the first time he had ever heard of someone possessing a fear of a common forest creature, albeit a humongous one.

"They're not natural," Cameron said. "They're like alien deer, sent here thousands of years ago by the overlords to lie waiting for the perfect time to overthrow humanity."

Devin chuckled. "Is that a scientific theory?"

Cameron shook his head rapidly. "No . . . just an idea."

"We should probably be on our way to that mountain," Nika said. "We've been out for a while now."

"Yes, excellent idea." Cameron brushed the grass from his knees and stood up. "Just as long as we steer clear of that thing, I'll be dandy."

"Don't worry," Trevor said. "I'm sure that moose is too busy plotting to take over the world to bother about us."

The temperature dropped significantly once the group arrived at the base of the waterfall. Instead of blistering heat, a biting chill laced the air, causing Trevor's skin to prickle from the cold. Nika shivered, hugging her arms close to her body and periodically reaching up to wipe the condensation from her visor.

"Looks deep," Cameron said, peering over the edge at a large pool of water gathering beneath the roaring waterfall. "I do hope these suits are waterproof." For some reason, Cameron wasn't showing any signs of discomfort. His voice was steady, and his body didn't tremble like the others'.

"Aren't you cold?" Trevor asked him.

A few rocks broke free from under Cameron's feet, falling into the pool, and he flung his arms out to catch his balance. "I don't usually get cold. My mom says it's my hyperactive blood, which is absurd, of course. Hyperactivity plays no role in the rising or dropping of body temperature." He laughed, evoking a slight smile from the otherwise reserved Nika.

"Is everyone still off-line?" Devin asked.

Trevor checked his visor and saw the bright red letters. "Yup." He whistled. "VIC? Can you hear us?"

No response.

Trevor squatted and dropped his gloved hand into the pool. The water was freezing cold, and he could feel it in his fingertips, despite the layer of neotanium shielding his skin. Rising to his feet, he wiped his hand on his thigh and examined the mountain.

"How do you explain all this water, Cameron?" Trevor

asked. "Did they build a gigantic swimming pool inside the Globe?"

Cameron sighed. "Must I explain everything?"

"You're the genius," Trevor said. "But with what you were saying earlier, this probably isn't even a real mountain, right?"

"Of course not." Cameron gave Trevor a sympathetic expression. "We're simply seeing a projection. That is most likely the inside wall of the Globe. Fine work indeed, but clearly not real."

"What do you think?" Nika asked Devin. "Do you agree with him?"

"I don't know, and I don't care about any of this," Devin said, his teeth chattering. "I just want to be done. We've made it to the waterfall, and VIC's not back online. I'm telling you, something's not right. How are we supposed to know where to go without help?"

Trevor couldn't understand why Devin was being so dramatic. So what if the adventure was going longer than expected? They could still have fun figuring things out on their own. "Maybe we're supposed to swim to the bottom of this pool, you know? Maybe there's like a secret passage we have to open while holding our breath."

"Oh, and you're going to dive down there to find out?" Devin sneered.

"Yeah, why not?"

"Well, it's freezing cold for starters, and . . ." Nika hesitated, averting her eyes from Trevor's. "I can't swim."

Trevor's face contorted into an expression of shock. "How is that possible? Aren't there pools in Russia?"

Nika glared. "Of course there are, and it's none of your business why I can't swim."

Cameron exhaled a loud sigh. "Well, that's a relief to me. Because I can't swim either. It's just too difficult working lessons into my busy summer schedule."

"Are you serious?" Trevor turned his attention to Devin, who held up his hands.

"Don't look at me. I can swim just fine," Devin said.

"Thank goodness!" Swimming was one of Trevor's favorite summer pastimes. He loved leaping from the top of the pool house into the deep end. When no one was paying attention, of course.

"But I'm not volunteering to dive into that frigid pond," Devin added.

"We could explore here first before someone swims to the bottom," Nika said. "Maybe there's something behind the waterfall. A room, perhaps, or a way through."

Nika was right. There was, in fact, a cave behind the waterfall. Ensconced on either side of the opening were flickering torches. Trevor wiggled his fingers through the flames and instantly felt searing heat as the moisture on his gloves sizzled.

"If that's *real* fire, then you'll probably ruin your suit by sticking it in there," Devin warned.

Something chirped in Trevor's helmet. It might have been static, but he could've sworn he heard a voice trying to come through. The word *off-line* disappeared for the briefest of blips before returning in the upper left corner of his visor. "I think VIC's trying to get through to us."

"First of all, VIC doesn't try anything. It's a computer. It either does or doesn't," Cameron said.

"You sound like Yoda," Devin said.

A wide smile stretched across Cameron's lips. "Really?"

Trevor moved past the torches and into the cave. Loud static once again crackled in his ears, accompanied by a few garbled words. "I bet you anything the reception out here is just really poor, and that if we go in there, we'll be able to hear through our helmets again."

But as they all began moving into the cave, Nika suddenly cried out. "Stop it!" she shouted in alarm. Devin had shoved her into Trevor and Cameron. She nearly fell, but managed to catch herself. "Don't push me!"

"Hurry!" Devin urged. "We have to go now!"

The ground began to shake as rubble dropped from overhead. Before Nika could protest any more, Devin pushed her completely through the opening, just as the ceiling collapsed behind him.

CHAPTER 19

THICK, HEAVY BOULDERS now completely blocked the cave's opening, shutting off the outside world and the torrential flow of the waterfall. Devin stumbled out of the way of a few falling rocks, searching the ceiling for signs of weakening. They were all lucky he'd acted when he did. Devin's premonition came within seconds of the actual roof collapse, and Nika would've suffered the worst of it. The vibration in Devin's chest subsided, and he scanned the room, checking on the others. Nika stood close by, less than a foot from the crumpled pile of stone. She was breathing heavily, but she looked to be okay. Cameron lay on top of Trevor, huddled in a ball.

"How did we end up on the ground?" Trevor asked, uncurling Cameron's body and pushing him to the side.

"I fell," Cameron mumbled.

"That's not how I remember it," Trevor said.

"That almost fell on us," Nika said, her shoulders quivering. She fixed Devin with an inquisitive gaze. "If you hadn't pushed us through when you did, we would've been crushed."

Devin shrugged. "Maybe. We just got lucky." He kicked a rock, sending it clacking across the stone floor.

Trevor stood, knocking away the film of dirt that had collected on his suit. "Yeah, how did you know it was going to collapse?"

Devin sniffed. "I heard a rumble."

"I think the rumble came after you shoved Nika into the cave," Trevor said. "Did you notice that the ceiling was about to fall?"

Devin looked up and shrugged. "Yeah, that's it. The ceiling was starting to break apart. That's why I pushed you in," he said in a monotone. But by the way Trevor stared at him, Devin knew he wasn't about to drop it.

"What about earlier, when we were in the cart, and you started freaking out about aborting the ride?" Trevor asked. "What was that all about?"

"I just wanted to get off the ride, okay? It's no big deal. Do you think there's a back door to this mountain?" he asked, wanting to change the subject.

Nika moved next to Trevor. "What are you not telling us, Devin?"

"Nothing, all right?" Devin glared at the both of them. "And you're welcome, for saving your lives. If I hadn't done anything, you all would've been buried."

"Devin's a clairvoyant!" Cameron suddenly burst out, hopping up and down excitedly. "I'm sorry!" He pressed his hands to the sides of his helmet and looked mournfully at Devin.

Devin groaned and clamped his eyes shut. He knew it was too much to hope that Cameron would just keep quiet. "You little snitch!" Devin hissed. "You said you wouldn't say anything."

"I know, but seeing how we're in this together now, I thought it would be good to share." He wiggled his fingers and scratched his armpits, tugging at the neotanium suit.

Devin swallowed and shifted his eyes to Trevor. What would he say now? Someone like Trevor would be a jerk about it. Devin knew plenty of kids just like him. Always trying to be funny.

"What does clairvoyant even mean?" Trevor asked.

Cameron's eyes almost bugged out of their sockets. "It's like he's a psychic—"

"Not a psychic," Devin snapped. "Don't look at me like I'm some freak." He whirled on Trevor and Nika, daring them to make a sound. "I don't read palms or burn weird candles. I just—" He sighed, glaring once more at Cameron. "It's called having a heightened sense of anticipation, okay? I can kind of see things before they happen. Sometimes." He stared at the floor and waited for the jokes to start.

"So you saw the ceiling collapse before it actually did?" Nika asked. "In your mind?"

Devin leaned his shoulder against the rock pile. "Yeah, sort of. It's easier when my mind's clear and not all fuzzy with everything else going on. I'm pretty spectacular when it comes to video games too."

"Video games?" Trevor asked with a spark in his eye.

"Yeah. They're much easier to figure out because they're preprogrammed, you know? I haven't played a game I couldn't beat in one sitting."

Trevor nodded. "Cool."

"Cool?" Devin studied Trevor's expression. "Or do you really mean weird?"

"Well, sure, weird, but not in a bad way," Trevor said. "I've seen commercials that show wild-eyed crazies saying they can see the future. But you don't match that description. So, it wasn't just a coincidence bumping into you the other night on the elevator, huh?"

Devin shook his head. "Not exactly."

"Why did you really want to abort the ride?" Nika asked. "What did you see about to happen?"

Devin looked away. "I don't know. That was different. It was some other type of feeling. I just knew that if we didn't abort the ride right then, something bad was going to happen."

"To you?" Cameron asked.

"Not necessarily. It could've been to any of us or none of us at all. It could've been to someone else." Devin puffed out his cheeks.

"An actual psychic?" Trevor gawked at him in disbelief.

"Don't call me that." Devin squared his shoulders, his hands clenching into fists. "No one was supposed to know."

"Then why did you tell loudmouth over here?" Trevor jabbed his thumb at Cameron.

"I didn't tell him. He came and found me last night in the arcade. Started jabbering about how he read all about me online." Devin narrowed his eyes at Cameron. "He probably knows something about each of us. Isn't that right?"

Cameron innocently pointed at his own chest.

"Yeah, you." Devin stepped toward him and pointed at Nika. "What can you tell us about her?"

Nika straightened and unfolded her arms.

Cameron swallowed. "Um, the Pushkins own several diamond mines in eastern Siberia."

Trevor stared at Nika, impressed. "Diamond mines?"

"So you've got money," Devin said.

"A little, I suppose," Nika said.

"Her grandfather has accrued several billion dollars'

worth of assets," Cameron added. "He's listed as one of the richest men in the world."

Nika's shoulders sagged. "Could you please not talk about my family's financial situation?"

Cameron sucked back on his teeth. "Sorry. It's hard for me to know when not to share."

Devin had never met an actual billionaire before. Nika acted normal enough. If Devin had that kind of money, he definitely wouldn't be wasting his time begging for followers on his YouTube channel. He would just own YouTube and be done with it.

"Why did you even enter the contest?" Devin asked.

Nika flinched. "What does that have to do with anything?"

"You could've just flown in and ridden whenever you wanted. But instead, you took the place of someone else. Someone who will probably never get a chance to try out the Adventure Machine."

"Hey, lay off her, man," Trevor said.

"Why? Because she's your girlfriend?" Devin sneered.

"No, because you're acting like a jerk. And it's not like you really care about being here either. You're just trying to become famous."

Nika laughed. "Is that why your dad is always filming? Is that why he tried to sneak a camera with you on the ride?"

"Shut up about my dad!" Devin said. "You don't know anything about him or me."

"Cameron does." Trevor pointed at Cameron.

Devin regarded Cameron with a look of contempt. "Just because he spends all day on his computer, looking people up. It's like you're a spy or something."

Cameron stepped away from Devin. "I'm sorry that I enjoy research, but I needed to know a little about everyone. It's not like you'd willingly share with me."

"Definitely not now that you've broken my trust," Devin said. If Cameron hadn't meddled, no one would have known. Now everything had changed. Devin hated being stared at, and even though they acted as though they didn't care about his condition, eventually one of them would say something. They would poke fun at him. Devin whirled on Cameron. "Why don't you spill the beans about Trevor too? Tell us his deep, dark secrets."

Trevor glanced over at Cameron, but Cameron simply hunched his shoulders.

"No," Cameron said quietly. "I never read anything about him."

"All right, let's take it easy on Cameron," Trevor said. "He's not trying to be a know-it-all. He just knows it all. And we need to work together to get out of here. Does anyone have any thoughts on how we do that?"

"I suppose we could start removing the rocks from the opening," Nika suggested.

"That seems like unnecessarily heavy work. Especially if we were intended to end up here to begin with," Cameron said, followed by a long, frustrated sigh. "Let's just think about this for a moment. VIC instructed us to go to the waterfall, which we did. But we didn't have any further directions, so we explored and discovered this secret passageway. That suggests to me that we're obviously in the exact spot where we should be."

"How did you come to that conclusion, Einstein?" Devin asked.

"Well, why would there be a need for a secret passageway on this ride? My guess is that it could be for one of two reasons, both of which should work in our favor. This is either part of our adventure and the roof collapse was intentional, to push us farther in, which I think is most likely the case . . ."

"And the second reason?" Trevor asked.

"This is some sort of service closet or a maintenance exit for workers to use to make their way in and out of the Globe." Cameron sniffed. "Personally, I would much rather it be that. I'm kind of growing tired with this whole ordeal."

"A service closet?" Nika questioned. "And then we just see what the ride wants us to see, correct? When in truth, there could be doors or regular lights on the ceiling, but it's covered with special effects."

"Precisely," Cameron said.

Devin frowned. "Why would they have special effects in a service closet?"

Cameron puckered his lips in thought. "Fine. Then we're sticking with my first choice, I guess. Either way, we're in the right spot."

"That actually does make sense," Devin said, easing his tone a bit. Maybe he had just overacted. It wouldn't have been the first time. "But I can't see a way out. It's too dark."

In an immediate response, the walls inside the cave began to emit a soft blue, phosphorescent glow. Devin's eyes rapidly adjusted to the change, and he noticed the source of the unusual light. Spongy mushrooms, the size of hubcaps, clung to the wall. The mushrooms pulsated as though alive, and with each deep, quivering breath, the light expanded to fill in the gaps of the mysterious cave.

"That's eerily convenient." Cameron squinted, leaning close to a nearby mushroom to examine it. "I wish lights went on whenever I commanded."

"Yeah, it's like the Clapper." Devin looked at Trevor, who stared back in confusion. "You know? Clap on, clap off, the Clapper? I watch old commercials on the Internet."

"And play tons of video games too, apparently," Trevor added.

Devin waggled his eyebrows. "And watch all sorts of scary movies."

"Like *Morlock of Mars*?" Trevor asked.

Devin shuddered. "Don't remind me."

Cameron poked the mushroom, and the light flickered. "With the manifestation of these radiating fungi, I think it's safe to say my theory was correct."

Nika stretched out a hand and gently patted Cameron's shoulder.

"What was that for?" Cameron asked.

"I guess it's nice to have you around," Nika said. "Like a good luck charm."

"Oh, well, okay." Cameron looked away.

Despite everything in the cave possessing a bluish tint, Devin could actually see the younger boy's cheeks flushing from embarrassment. As annoying as Cameron could be with his constant barrage of data and unsolicited statistics, Devin agreed with Nika. It was great to have him along for the ride. He decided he would give the others the benefit of the doubt.

"Sorry, guys," Devin mumbled. "I kind of freaked out back there. It's just . . . my dad spends so much time on his phone. He's always filming me. Telling me to act a certain way. When I realized I lost it, I knew I was in big trouble and I just blew everything out of proportion."

"We'll all tell him that it wasn't your fault," Cameron said. "The sheer velocity of the Adventure Machine made it impossible to maintain a grasp on any accessories."

Devin smiled at Cameron. "I think I know what you just said."

Trevor playfully slugged Devin in the shoulder. "Don't worry about it. Seriously, Devin, we'll stick together on this. Your dad will understand. And there will be tons of interviews after we get off the ride that you can use on your channel."

"It's not just that," Devin said. He sighed. "I don't think I even want to have my own channel. I mean, it was cool at first. The idea of becoming famous. But that was before my dad went all crazy filming everything. He's always sneaking up on me and trying to knock my drink off the table or jump out from closets and surprise me."

"Why would he do that?" Nika looked appalled. "My grandfather strictly forbids anyone to sneak up on me."

Devin shrugged. "My dad wants to show the world just how accurate my *ability* can be. He wants to show everyone how cool it is to be psychic. He thinks we'll get super rich."

"It *is* cool," Trevor said. "I wish I were psychic."

"Yeah, well, it may be cool at times, but I don't think I'm ready for my face to be out there all over the Internet as the kid who can see the future. You don't know what it's like to be a freak." No one ever understood. Devin always feared that one day he would be doing a routine checkup at the doctor's, and then he'd never get to go home. He'd spend the rest of his life under the microscope.

Nika looked away from Devin and stared at her feet. "I kind of know how you feel."

"You do?" Devin asked, studying Nika. She was acting strange. Distant. As if she wanted to tell them something, but didn't have the words for it.

"We should probably find a way out of here," she said after a moment's hesitation.

"Yeah," Trevor agreed. "We just have to keep telling ourselves that this is all part of the adventure. If we do that, we'll be fine. Just remember that we're supposed to be here."

"But you're not supposed to be here," a voice spoke from inside their helmets.

Devin froze, listening. The voice didn't sound as if it belonged to VIC or anyone else he knew.

"You heard that too, didn't you?" Trevor asked, narrowing his eyes in concentration. Nika tilted her head slightly to one side to listen.

"This is not part of the ride," the voice continued. It sounded garbled and inhuman. Not a smooth, calming voice like the one VIC used, or the grinding robotic drone of the Ganglion, but more like that of a croaking bullfrog.

"What do you mean by that?" Devin asked, moving closer to the group until the four of them stood within inches of each other.

"You were invited to this room for a reason. A reason some would not want you to know about." From the far corner of the cave, something dropped from the ceiling. It landed gracefully, producing hardly a thud against the stone floor.

Trevor took a few steps toward the figure crouching in the shadows beneath a particularly enormous, pulsating mushroom.

"Stay where you are, Trevor," the voice insisted, as the thing in the corner hissed menacingly.

"Why?" Trevor asked. "What is that?"

"What am I? I, like you, am something that shouldn't be here," the voice clarified. "I was put here by my creator to serve a purpose."

"The voice is coming from that *thing*!" Devin whispered. "This is freaking me out. How does it know your name?"

"I've been programmed to know each of you and to deliver a message." The figure in the corner straightened to its full height, which was slightly taller than Cameron.

Dressed in a tattered uniform with odd-looking medals and thick-soled combat boots, the figure was definitely not human. In fact, Devin thought it resembled some sort of lizard. A gecko perhaps, with two bulging eyes moving independently of each other.

"Do not come closer. Do not touch me," the lizard thing instructed, though it never opened its mouth or moved its lips when it talked. Instead, its words continued to pour out from inside their helmets.

"Don't aggravate it," Cameron pleaded.

Trevor held up his hands in a nonthreatening display. "I wasn't going to touch him."

"It's obviously some sort of soldier, judging by the way it's dressed," Cameron said. "Which means it could attack us."

"You are a virus. All of you," the lizard said. "Your touch will destroy me and my message."

"Then what's your message?" Devin demanded.

One of the lizard's eyes swiveled and focused in on Devin. A mushroom adhered to the wall beside the pile of toppled stone suddenly swelled to twice its original size and began to buzz. Then the phosphorescent light flickered off, like a faulty lightbulb. The creature looked alarmed.

"How were you chosen?" the lizard asked, blinking solemnly.

"What does that mean?" Devin asked. "Do you mean for the ride?"

It nodded.

"We entered a contest," Nika said. "We were randomly selected."

A clucking sound began to rise from the creature's throat. At first, Devin thought the lizard was choking, but then he realized that it was actually laughing, emitting a low, methodical chuckle. "Your selection was not random," it said. "The contest is a farce. You are special. Only you can make it work. Only you can break it. You are being stolen!" The lizard's voice echoed in Devin's helmet. "Can't you feel it? Don't you see? The Adventure Machine is not what it seems!"

Nika brushed up against Devin's arm. "I don't think this is meant to be part of the ride," she whispered.

It was almost as if the four of them had slipped into a glitch in the system. Something not part of the Adventure Machine's original programming.

"We are being stolen?" Cameron asked. "Explain what that means."

"No time. I have already been discovered and will be vanquished soon," the lizard said.

One by one, the other mushrooms in the cave did the same as the first, buzzing, flickering, and then dimming until the once-bright light had all but vanished. "Someone on the inside has corrupt intentions," the lizard continued. Only the mushroom directly above him remained, and it too had begun to buzz. "They will do all that they can to stop you. You must end this. Do it now before it's too late!"

The lizard's eyes swiveled once more. When the voice spoke again, it came across distorted. Devin could barely pick out the words in between fits of ear-piercing static. He could, however, hear a different voice struggling to break through. The sound had grown so loud and sharp, Devin wanted to yank his helmet from his head and toss it aside. He clamped his eyes shut from the pain, but then it stopped. When he opened them, the only mushroom left lit in the cave gave one final flicker, and the uniformed lizard vanished. The room plunged once more into darkness, but only for a fleeting moment. Then a new light appeared where the creature once stood.

It was a bright red Exit sign.

CHAPTER 20

ARTIFICIAL LIGHT POURED in as Cameron poked his head through the exit, twisting from left to right as he examined the track. "That's impossible," he muttered.

The Adventure Machine cart rested on the opposite side of the exit door, balancing at the peak of a sloping stretch. Above Cameron, security lights dotted an expansive section of curved wall that towered hundreds of feet in the air. He could see the winding metal track like the skeletal remains of an enormous dinosaur, looming all around. "It must be a duplicate. Our vehicle went miles and miles in the opposite direction."

Trevor approached the cart. He picked up one of the teth-ered abort remotes and waved it in the air. "It's definitely our ride. These are scattered all over the place, except for the one beneath my seat. Just how we left them."

Cameron remained in the doorway, keeping his foot wedged beneath the door to prevent it from closing. Just in case. Not that the damp mountain was by any means ideal. With that peculiar lizard and the glowing fungi, Cameron doubted an actual safe place existed inside the Globe. Still, the Adventure Machine cart almost certainly spelled complete disaster. "What just happened?"

"We got out of there," Devin answered. "And it's about time, if you ask me."

"Am I the only one worried about what that lizard said?" Cameron asked. "It told us that we were being stolen. And that someone was corrupt. I'm thinking that refers to someone who works on or operates the Adventure Machine."

Devin, who'd already climbed into the cart, rapped his knuckles on the back of the seat. "What does it want with us?"

"I'm thinking it's not really us this person wants to steal, but our abilities," Cameron said.

"But I'm the only one with an ability. What, does he or she want to be psychic? I mean clairvoyant?"

Cameron glared at Devin. "Don't forget, I'm a genius."

Trevor glanced sideways at Cameron. "Yes, we know."

"I don't mean that in a condescending way," Cameron said, growing impatient. Honestly, talking with middle school children could be quite taxing at times. You had to spell everything out in simple terms. Cameron may have been a year or two younger than the three of them, but only in age. "I'm a genius because of a medical condition I've had since birth. Hyperactive ingenuity. Due to this condition, my intellect has been able to accelerate."

"Okay, so there's two of us, then," Devin said. "Big deal."

Cameron pursed his lips and sighed. Devin's reaction earlier had been less than favorable, but the circumstances in the Adventure Machine had drastically changed. Everyone needed to know all the facts. Cameron nodded at Trevor expectantly. "Don't you feel it's time to clue everyone in? There's nothing to be ashamed of. Your condition is quite impressive."

Devin looked at Trevor and then back at Cameron. "Seriously? *He* has a special ability? What is it? He knows how to annoy people really well?" Devin snickered, and Trevor smiled, playing along.

"No, Trevor was born with a misfiring amygdala," Cameron explained.

Devin made a worried expression. "Yikes. Sorry, man. That sounds bad."

Cameron groaned, wishing he had something to throw. Not that he would actually throw it at Devin. The guy might have been naive, but Cameron barely stood midway past Devin's belly button. "It means he was born absolutely fearless."

Devin gnawed on his lower lip and prepared to grin, as though waiting for the punchline. "Bull," he said. "No way. Fearless?"

Trevor shrugged. "I'm afraid so." Then he laughed. "Get it? Afraid?"

Devin reclined in his chair. "Sorry, but I don't buy that for one second."

"I believe it." Nika had been quiet since Cameron started up the discussion, but now she looked at Trevor with a sort of subtle admiration. "When we were in space, you tried to touch the comet. You were going to do it, weren't you?"

"Maybe not," Trevor said, shrugging.

Cameron leaned against the door in the entryway. "So you see? My intellect, Devin's clairvoyance, Trevor's fearlessness. That makes three of us with conditions worth stealing."

Nika sighed. "Four of us."

Cameron clapped his hands. "I knew it! I just knew there had to be something special about you. You're very good at keeping it hidden, though, and off-line."

"Well?" Trevor asked Nika.

"Yeah, what makes you so special?" Devin swiveled in his seat to face her.

Nika pressed her lips together before speaking. "I have a condition called congenital insensitivity."

Cameron's eyes lit up. "Oh my!" What an amazing find! Congenital insensitivity? And that did explain some things.

And yet, that didn't thoroughly explain Nika's unusual behavior. She behaved as though she was afraid of any contact whatsoever. Had living with her condition that long changed her responses to normal situations?

"What does that mean?" Devin asked.

"I don't feel pain," she said. "My body doesn't produce that sensation at all."

Trevor was shocked. "That's pretty cool," he said. "Why do you seem so sad about it? If I had your ability, I'd celebrate."

Nika's eyes opened rapidly, and she looked up at Trevor. "It is not cool. It is horrible. I never know when I am injured. I never know if I've done something bad to myself, and no one ever understands. They always tell me that they wished they had my condition." She gritted her jaw. "But they don't know what they're talking about."

The four of them fell into an awkward silence as Nika folded her arms and stared at the floor. After a moment, Cameron cleared his throat. "The lizard said we should end this. How can we . . . End what?"

"Couldn't it just be that this is part of our adventure?" Devin asked. "Maybe we're all freaking out for no reason."

"I do think it was strange how Doug came to my home to convince my grandfather to let me come here," Nika said. "Why did he have to convince him? Either I could participate or not. If we refused, there were countless other children who could've taken my place. I was so excited to have a chance for a real adventure, I didn't take the time to wonder how he knew about me when hardly anyone does."

"Tell me about it," Cameron said. "You're a mystery, to be certain."

"He came to my house too," Devin said.

"So the whole contest was just a fake?" Trevor asked. "A way to lure us out here to ride the Adventure Machine?"

Cameron allowed the door to close behind him and slowly approached the cart. "Not a fake. Just rigged. They would have had to be very careful because the media was involved. If they caught wind of treachery on the part of the Castletons, they could've exposed it to the world. A mistake like that could shut down the ride forever."

"Why would they not just ask us to come?" Trevor wondered. "Why take the risk?"

Cameron sighed. "Now, that I don't know. But he is Doug Castleton. A bold risk-taker by nature."

Nika waited patiently for Cameron to climb back in, and then she carefully swung her leg over the side of the cart. At the exact moment she slid into her seat, thick smoke suddenly began pouring out from the hood. It vented and spat, and Cameron was about to leap from the train, when another loud crackle of static echoed through their helmets.

"How's everyone holding up?"

"Is that VIC?" Devin asked, elevating his voice above the sound of the venting hood.

"No need to shout," VIC answered. "I can hear you loud and clear."

Trevor peered across the cone of the cart at the cloud. "Where did you go? And why are we smoking?"

VIC chuckled, his robotic voice growing slightly distorted. "As I'm sure you're well aware, the Adventure Machine has had a breakdown. We'll have you back on track in a few minutes."

"Breakdown?" Trevor asked, climbing into his seat. "We just got back in the cart."

"If you would remain in your seats until a fix can be issued, that would be swell," VIC continued. "Please keep your helmets on for your own protection." Another bout of static filled Cameron's ears. He cringed, clamping his hands to the sides of his helmet.

Trevor nudged Cameron's arm. "Is VIC malfunctioning or something?"

"I don't think VIC knows we got out of the cart," Cameron whispered.

"How could he not know?" Devin asked, keeping his voice low. "He was the one who told us to exit, remember?"

Nika leaned forward. "Unless that wasn't really VIC," she said. "What if what we thought was VIC was really someone else trying to direct us toward the cave and that lizard."

Cameron nodded at Nika. Those were his thoughts exactly, which added to his growing suspicion about the Adventure Machine. Cameron held his finger up to his visor and shushed the others. "Don't reveal anything to VIC. Just keep quiet and see how this plays out."

More static erupted from Cameron's helmet. "I should be able to discover a way to reboot your vehicle in no time," VIC said.

Cameron stiffened in his seat. "Before you get us rolling, I think it would be more critical to fix our seat belts. There's no way to latch them in place. You know this, I presume?"

"Good call," Devin said, slipping his arms under the straps and making yet another attempt to fasten the buckle. "That would've been bad."

"Ah, yes," VIC said, followed by yet another piercing round of static. Cameron wanted badly to yank his helmet off and cover his ears. "Have you tried resetting the locking mechanism on your safety harnesses?"

"How do we do that?" Nika asked. "That wasn't explained to us."

"It's quite simple. There's a lever on the underside of the latch where you insert the harness buckle. Just push that down, and you should hear it click. After that, the harness should be operational once more."

Cameron located the lever and followed VIC's instructions. The others did the same, but unfortunately, the procedure didn't work. None of their harnesses would buckle into the latch.

"Interesting," VIC said. "Give me just a few moments to assess this."

A soft hum began to vibrate through the base of the train. Though it was hardly noticeable at first, Cameron could feel it gaining strength.

"All right," VIC announced. "It appears that more than a minor malfunction has occurred with the Adventure Machine's wiring. At present, I can't restart your vehicle."

Cameron rested his hand on his seat cushion. "But I can feel it buzzing as if we're still holding a charge."

"The electrical conduit within the track is still live. It's programmed to recycle periodically and can do so without causing any disruption, even when the ride is operating. When the train went off-line, it must have coincided with the recycle. What you're feeling now is normal."

Cameron looked over the side down at the tubular track beneath them. "If we're live, won't that be dangerous to touch?"

"Not for you. You'll maintain an electrical ground as long as you continue wearing your neotanium suits," VIC explained.

"Great. So we won't get shocked, but we can't go anywhere," Devin said.

"On the contrary," VIC said. "It just so happens vector seven, where your train is currently stationed, is conveniently positioned on the apex of a *tumble*."

"Of a what?" Trevor asked.

"A tumble is not quite steep enough to be labeled as a hill. Approximately forty feet down this tumble, the track levels off and connects with a solid platform just before plunging down the Palisade, a three-hundred-and-thirty-foot drop," VIC said. "At the base of the tumble, there's a section of switch rail, which will allow the train to go off track to a safe workstation. To remedy your current predicament, one would simply need to descend the tumble and engage the switch rail's release mechanism."

Trevor glanced around at the others, his forehead crinkling in confusion. "What is he talking about?"

"I think VIC wants someone to climb down the track," Nika said. "But there's no way my grandfather would ever approve of such a plan. We could slip and fall."

"My mom either," Cameron added.

What VIC was suggesting didn't feel like a reasonable option. Instructing children to chance falling down a forty-foot drop was borderline lunacy.

"Is there a harness?" Cameron asked.

"No harnesses," VIC immediately replied. More disruptive static followed his voice. It increased in volume and then fizzled. VIC's voice transmission ended as the off-line message appeared in the upper left-hand corner of Cameron's visor.

Cameron smacked the side of his helmet. "Off-line again? Why is everything breaking down?"

Nika ran her fingers down her safety strap and cautiously peered over the edge. "Maybe it has something to do with what happened before," she said softly. "Maybe it's because we witnessed something we shouldn't have."

Cameron whirled around. "My thoughts exactly!" The lizard had said that the ride would try to stop them. By Cameron's calculations, the Adventure Machine was doing a pretty impressive job so far.

"So what then?" Devin asked. "It's been like at least forty-five minutes. Doug said the ride would only take a half an hour at the most. Should we just sit here and wait for them to come get us?"

"No way am I going to sit here and wait forever while this machine tries to figure things out." Trevor stood and leaned over the front of the hood. "I'll just climb down and hit the switch. It looks wide enough to use as a ladder."

Cameron frowned. "It's forty feet to the bottom."

"I'll be fine." Trevor swung his left leg over the far side of the cart. Cameron, along with the others, reached out and snagged him by different sections of his uniform, forcing him back into his seat. Trevor hit the padded cushion with a thud and expelled a loud "Oof!"

"Are you crazy?" Nika hissed.

"You almost jumped over the side," Cameron said. "A fall from this high would've proven costly. Maybe even fatal."

"Geez, sorry." Trevor shrugged away their hands and looked down to where he had almost leapt.

"Just stop being so impulsive," Nika muttered. "Think before you make a foolish decision. What if you had fallen? One of us would've had to find a way down to you. Or we would've had to wait for someone to come, and you would be lying there probably dying for over an hour."

Cameron drummed his fingers on his knee. "Engaging the switch rail won't be enough. Not if our cart is immobile." He cautiously stood, examining the cart's cone and noticing a thin line where the hood disconnected from the rest of the vehicle. "We'll need to manually override the brake somehow and slip us into neutral."

"Can you do that?" Devin asked.

Cameron bobbled his head. "Probably. But I'll need help removing the control panel."

Nika glanced warily at Trevor. "Are we just going to let him go through with this?"

"Look, I'm not going to fall. I know how to climb down a ladder," Trevor said.

Cameron sighed. As much as he hated to admit it, Trevor's plan seemed like the only feasible option. "If somehow the Adventure Machine goes back online, who's to know if the safety harnesses will ever reengage? We'll be stuck in this death trap and plummeting down three hundred feet into the pits!" The sooner Trevor flipped that switch, the better.

"I agree with the little guy." Devin nodded at Cameron and then glanced at Trevor. "Just don't fall, okay?"

"Yes, be careful," Nika said. "I liked it much better when I didn't know you were clinically fearless."

"Fearless doesn't mean stupid," Trevor said.

Cameron watched as Trevor's foot slipped and his stomach smacked against the hood. Shooting out his hands, Trevor grappled to find a hold on something. Cameron covered his visor, peering through the slats between his fingers, horrified that gravity was about to suck Trevor into the void.

"That was an accident, okay?" Trevor said, as he caught the thin edge of metal beneath the front console and steadied himself from falling.

Something in Cameron's stomach gurgled. He assumed it was an ulcer. A right big one, at that. He slowly lowered his hands and held his breath as Trevor began shinnying his way down below the cart.

CHAPTER 21

NIKA STOOD AND watched as Devin helped Cameron pop up a square section of metal on the nose of the cart. She felt a cold tingle travel through her shoulders. Normally, she didn't mind a tingling, which was one of the only sensations she could feel, due to her congenital insensitivity. But at that moment, Nika didn't appreciate the change in temperature. The malfunctioning machine didn't appear to be an accident. It felt rigged, as if something was trying to prevent them from escaping. If what the lizard said was true, and there was indeed someone corrupt working behind the scenes of the Adventure Machine, they might purposely place Nika and her new friends in danger.

Craning her neck, Nika attempted to see if she could spot

Trevor's helmet as he descended, but it was no use. The position of the train made it impossible to see anything below. Trevor seemed nice and easy to talk to, but he also could be rash and clumsy, and he definitely embraced his fearless ability. What would that be like? Nika wondered. To not have to worry? To volunteer first for a dangerous task without any care about what could happen?

When each of them had revealed their conditions to the group, Nika had been partially honest. Congenital insensitivity was a real thing that impacted her life. But it wasn't the only issue. No one, other than her family and the Castletons, knew of her real problem. The disease that made her live her life in a bubble. Always protected. Always forbidden to do normal everyday activities. Riding the Adventure Machine was the single most dangerous thing she had ever done.

Nika shifted uncomfortably. "Have you figured it out yet?"

"There appears to be some sort of circuit box next to the main engine drive," Cameron grunted as he wedged his hand under a web of metal tubing. "I can see it, but I can't get my fingers around the wing nuts locking it."

"Don't look at me," Devin said. "You've got smaller hands than I do. Wouldn't it be so much easier if we could do this without our suits?"

"Easier yes," Cameron said. "But the neotanium suit is the only thing standing between our skin and over two hundred amps of electrical current. A one hundredth of that amount could stop our hearts."

"That would be shocking." Devin offered Cameron a smile.

Cameron emitted another grunt, followed by a full squeal of joy as he managed to unscrew the wing nuts and open the box. "Okay, one of these wires should flip the cart into neutral. The question is which one?"

"I know you're a genius, but how do you know so much?" Nika asked. It wasn't just scientific data with Cameron. The boy seemed to know everything about everything.

"I read a few roller coaster manuals before our trip out here to the facility."

"You mean within the last week?"

Cameron nodded. "Uh-huh. Fascinating material!"

"Ever think of watching a movie instead?" Devin asked.

"Like a movie on roller-coaster manuals?" Cameron looked intrigued. "Do they make such a thing? I would definitely make time for a show like that."

"Uh, never mind." Devin glanced back at Nika and grinned. "Forget I asked."

"Yes, maybe you should just focus on the task at hand." Nika peered over Cameron's shoulder at the four crinkled wires jutting out from a row of plastic ports. Each wire was a different color. "What else could the wires be controlling?"

Cameron wiggled his fingers and nibbled on his lower lip. "Now that, I'm not one hundred percent certain on."

"Could disconnecting any of them make us fall off the track?" Devin asked.

Cameron giggled. "Of course not! Why would that be an option?"

"Then just yank them all out," Devin said.

Cameron opened his mouth to protest but curled his lip. "You know, you're right." With a quick jerk of his hand, he pulled the four wires free from their ports.

Nika felt a sudden jolt beneath her feet, and she nearly stumbled. "I think the cart can move now." She cautiously lowered herself into her seat, careful not to make any jarring movements, and once against fitted her arms beneath the harness.

"It would appear so," said Cameron. "Now it will only require a slight prod from behind to send us down this tumble."

Devin held his hands out for balance. "But we don't want to do that just yet."

"Why not?" Cameron asked.

"Because Trevor hasn't switched us over," Nika said. "We'll run over him on our drop down the Palisade."

Cameron shook his index finger emphatically. "I'm certainly glad we're working together on this."

Nika flinched as a melodious chime sounded in her ears.

"Hello once again," VIC suddenly announced. She exhaled in relief. Hearing the familiar voice of the ride's virtual tour guide brought her a sense of comfort.

"You're back," Devin said.

"I'm back," VIC answered.

"Have you fixed our seat belt situation?" Nika asked.

"No," VIC said, a hint of regret in his robotic voice. "But three of your heart rates are slightly elevated, though the cart is currently out of order. Would you care for some soothing tunes to calm your senses?"

"You can play music?" Devin asked.

"Of course. What song would you like me to play?"

A slight grin formed on Devin's lips. "Do you have any heavy metal?"

"That would not be considered soothing, or recommended," VIC said. "I do have a wide selection of instrumental classics and golden oldies. Would you prefer Bach, Beethoven, Mozart, the Doobie Brothers . . . *Danger. Incoming.*" VIC paused briefly.

Cameron scowled. "Danger. Incoming? I've never heard of them."

"Incoming," VIC repeated, more forcibly.

It wasn't a song option. VIC was issuing a warning.

Nika was the first to notice the shadowy figure dangling from the upper track before it dropped from above and landed with a clang of metal, less than ten yards behind the cart.

The three kids and VIC fell silent. Nika felt her pulse quicken as she studied the darkness, but the figure remained hidden among the shadows cast by the security lights.

"What is that?" Cameron whispered. "Is that someone coming to help us?"

"No, that is not," VIC answered. "The Castletons and your guardians are more than forty-seven miles of track away in the control room, oblivious to your current predicament."

"They don't know that we've broken down?" Nika asked, desperation rising in her voice.

"Of course not," VIC said. "The Adventure Machine has not made any indication of the ride's status or malfunctions. That particular data will not be available until after the ride's completion."

"Okay, then what's that?" Devin pointed into the shadows.

"*That* is number three."

"Number three of what?" Cameron squeaked.

"Number three of six," VIC explained.

The virtual ride companion wasn't making any sense to Nika. Was this more technical jargon? That only Cameron could understand?

"Remain calm," VIC instructed. "Do not make any

sudden movements, and wait for my command. I will devise a way to avoid a confrontation with the creature."

"Creature?" Nika fixed her eyes to the spot just beyond the light's reach. She held her breath as a figure stepped into the light.

Devin swallowed and hunched in his seat. "I think I know what that is."

"Yes, Mr. Drobbs," VIC said. "It is now imperative that you do exactly as I say."

CHAPTER 22

TREVOR SLIPPED ONLY once more on his way to the bottom of the tumble. He accidentally misjudged the lower divots, forcing him to dangle by his fingertips for a couple of seconds as he probed the track with his feet for another foothold. He waited for someone to shout at him for being impulsive or irresponsible. When it didn't happen, Trevor figured he was far enough down that the others couldn't see his progress. After that near mishap, it was pretty much smooth sailing to the platform below.

At just over six feet in diameter, the platform gave Trevor plenty of room to stretch his legs. Just as VIC had instructed, Trevor easily found the adjacent track, which, with the press of some button, would send the cart veering to the right of the main line and drop to yet another, even longer, platform. A hallway, lit up with more of the safety lights, connected with the center of the platform, and at the end of that, Trevor could see the faint glow of a Maintenance sign.

"I'm here," Trevor announced. "What now?" He waited for an answer, but none came. "Hello?"

The crackle of static was the only reply.

"Figures," he grumbled. Leaning against the guardrail, Trevor moved over and stood next to a keypad embedded in the rail. Along with ten numbers, the keypad had two circular buttons: red and green.

"Just tell me which one to push." Trevor didn't want to wait any longer. Green had to mean go, and he assumed that meant the train would continue on its normal course. Therefore, red might mean stop, or in this case, a way to divert the cart to the maintenance track. Or maybe it was the other way around. The green button could possibly indicate "go" to the new track, which made the decision slightly more complicated. Trevor placed his index finger on the green button but didn't press it. If he didn't hear from VIC within the next thirty seconds, he would make his own decision and live with the consequences. Green seemed like the more exciting choice.

"Red or green," Trevor announced. "If you don't tell me what to do, I'm going to . . ." He stopped before finishing.

Someone was sitting in the maintenance hallway, watching him.

No, not someone. Some . . . *thing.*

Trevor leaned forward, squinting. "Hey there," he said. "Who are you?" As his eyes adjusted, Trevor realized what he was seeing.

It was one of the creatures he had met in the warehouse the other night with Devin. It crouched, insect-like, on its four limbs in the nearby corridor. Its eyes, like distant, burning stars, stared, expressionless, at Trevor. With all the fun on the Adventure Machine, Trevor had almost forgotten all about them.

"How long have you been down there?" he asked the creature.

The creature stiffened and bolted upright in alarm. Standing at full height, it looked to be easily seven feet tall, perhaps even eight feet, with a thin, spindly body, but really no musculature that Trevor could see. Its mantis-like head was a jagged trapezoid, forming two distinct points on either side, which may have been its ears. When Trevor had his first encounter with One, he remembered how lifeless and inhuman its eyes seemed. But now he noticed distinct pupils quivering amid yellowish glowing orbs.

Trevor held up his hands, trying to calm it. "Don't be afraid. I won't hurt you." Scaring it away was the last thing he wanted to happen. "Have I met you before?" He kept his voice as smooth and nonthreatening as he could manage.

The creature hesitated, but then nodded.

"Are you . . . One?" Trevor asked, growing excited.

It nodded again.

Standing out in the open, away from the confines of its pod, One looked even more strikingly similar to the alien Morlock. In fact he felt certain, had the two been standing side by side, he wouldn't be able to tell them apart. Maybe his creator was a movie buff.

"How did you get over there?"

One cocked his head and then looked down at his feet. Just below the platform, Trevor could make out what looked like a ladder scaling down the side.

"Cool," Trevor said. "Where are your other friends from the pods?"

The creature took a moment to process the question, before holding out his palms, indicating that he didn't know.

"So you're all alone. Like me. Well, I'm not entirely alone. My friends are still up there." Trevor pointed to the top of the tumble, and One timidly followed his finger. "I'm trying to figure out which button to push on this doohickey here. Our cart broke down and needs fixing. You don't know, do you?"

One nodded a third time, almost immediately.

"Really?" Trevor asked in surprise. "Okay, so there are

two buttons. Red and—" One held up his claw to stop Trevor from continuing. "Red?"

One held up a long, slender thumb. Trevor laughed. Did the creature actually know the meaning of a thumbs-up?

Trevor moved his finger off the green button and over to the red one, and pushed it in. The track next to his feet produced a languid clank as it slid over and connected with the piece leading down to the other platform.

"That did it!" Trevor looked over to thank the creature, but One had vanished. There was no sign of him anywhere. "Where did you go?" He glanced at the ladder, wondering if One had climbed back down. Instead of any sort of response, Trevor heard something else. It sounded like oncoming traffic.

Trevor looked up just in time to dive out of the way of the Adventure Machine as it whooshed down the tumble at full speed.

CHAPTER 23

THE ADVENTURE MACHINE connected with the adjacent track and slammed headfirst into a rubber bumper at the end of the maintenance platform. The sound of crunching metal filled the narrow corridor as the cart's nose collapsed like an accordion.

"Are you kidding me?" Trevor gaped down at the wreckage in disbelief.

Fluids seeped out of the train from no less than a hundred open wounds. Hissing smoke gushed, and both rear wheels had rolled away from their axles.

Trevor hurriedly climbed down the adjacent piece of track and raced over to find Nika and Cameron still seated inside the cart. Devin, on the other hand, clung to the back, his fingers gripping one of the safety harnesses as his feet dangled over the edge. All three of them gulped deep breaths of air, and tears gushed from Nika's eyes.

"I kind of thought you guys would wait for me to come back up before you shoved off," Trevor said.

Nika pulled herself out of the cart and ran her hands up and down her arms as if searching for injuries. She crouched behind the Adventure Machine, scanning the upper platform. Cameron slithered over the side like a worm. He plopped on the ground and rolled away from the cart, trying to hide next to the wall.

Trevor glanced at Devin, who had pried his fingers from the safety harness and now joined Nika behind the cart. "What are you guys doing?"

"Get down!" Devin ordered. "It'll see you."

Trevor turned around, trying to spot what had all of them spooked. "What will see me?"

"VIC says it's still up there," Nika whispered.

Trevor smacked the side of his helmet. "When did your helmets start working again?" Nika, Devin, and Cameron started backing away from the cart, moving toward the exit. "Would somebody please tell me what's going on?" Trevor demanded.

"Once we're out of this place, we'll tell you," Nika said.

Just beyond the exit door, they discovered a room that appeared to be in a state of disrepair. Wires and conduits cascaded down from several missing ceiling tiles, as did fluffy chunks of fiberglass insulation. Trevor saw an extension ladder lying on its side next to several cans of paint. There were paint rollers and pans and overturned buckets. A few folding chairs circled a table where someone had stretched out a set of construction blueprints on the counter. A low-wattage lightbulb hung at the center of the ceiling, dimly lighting the small room. In the far corner, Trevor noticed another door, blocked by a skeletal section of scaffolding.

As soon as Trevor walked into the room, Devin pulled him the rest of the way through, then slammed the door shut and locked the dead bolt.

"What's gotten into you guys?" Trevor plopped down in one of the metal chairs and ran his fingers across the blueprint, coming up with a glove full of dust. He didn't have much experience in reading blueprints, but he felt fairly certain that the one laid out on the table was a detailed floor plan of the rooms and hallways surrounding the Globe.

Devin leaned back against the door with his hand firmly on the doorknob. "One of the creatures from the other night just tried to kill us." His heavy breathing had fogged up the inside of his visor.

"What do you mean 'the other night'?" Cameron asked.

It took Trevor a second to locate Cameron, who had managed to shimmy behind the extension ladder and was now holding one of the paint rollers outstretched like a weapon.

"Last night, Trevor and I snuck out of our rooms and went exploring on the bottom floor."

Cameron looked at Trevor in shock. "You snuck out? You said you weren't going to go."

"Well, I changed my mind." Trevor shrugged. "It's no big deal."

"And you invited Devin and not me?"

"Okay, stop," Devin said. "That's not the point. We saw those creatures growing inside these pods. Trevor was trying to show off and started communicating with one of them and probably ticked it off."

"That's not at all what happened," Trevor said. "And One wasn't aggressive. In fact, I just spoke with him not thirty seconds before you nearly ran me off the road. He helped me switch the track over."

"Are you speaking in another language?" Cameron squeaked. "One what?"

"The creature's name is One," Trevor explained.

Nika eased into one of the chairs and placed her trembling hands on the table. She seemed more concerned about something else, something unrelated to her close encounter with a terrifying creature.

"You all just overreacted for no reason. Just like with that moose," Trevor said, turning to Cameron.

"VIC was the one who told us to get out of there," Cameron said. "We were just following instructions."

Running his fingers along the base of his helmet, Trevor found where he could unlatch it from his suit. Before anyone could stop him, he pulled it off with a soft pop, and placed it on the table. "Mine's not working," he explained when he was met with looks of outrage.

"But you're not supposed to remove your helmet," Cameron said. "You won't be fully protected."

Trevor swiveled the helmet around so that he could see through the visor. "I doubt it even works anymore."

A sudden hollow knock thudded against the door. Devin yelped and leapt out of the way. Nika stood from her seat, and Cameron brandished the spongy roller once again for protection, milky white paint dripping at his side.

"What do we do?" Cameron's voice rose in panic.

"Let's open it," Trevor suggested.

"Oh yeah, because that's a smart idea," Devin whispered, backing away from the door.

"It may just be me, but that didn't sound like a monster knocking," Trevor said.

Another knock and then: "Hello? Is anyone in there? This is Terry Castleton."

"See?" Trevor said, pointing at the door.

Devin wasn't convinced. "How do we know it's really you?"

"I'm not sure how to answer that," Terry said. "But I do

feel that's kind of an odd question to ask. Who else would I be?"

Satisfied, Devin cautiously unlocked the door and pulled it open.

"Okay, good," Terry said, pressing his hand against his chest and performing a quick head count of everyone in the room. Like the others, he wore a Cerebral Apparatus, complete with a matching helmet. But unlike theirs, Terry's helmet had a pair of headlamps adhered to the sides of it, next to his visor. Though small, the lights were bright enough to cause Trevor to shield his eyes. When Terry noticed Trevor's discomfort, he gave a quick verbal command to VIC, who immediately extinguished the lights.

"Sorry about that. It's quite dark out there, don't you agree? And the track can be tricky to negotiate." Terry also wore a belt around his waist with a zippered pouch like some sort of fanny pack. "I must say, when I didn't see you up on the track, I had a moment of panic. Then I saw the demolished cart on the maintenance platform." He raised an eyebrow in disappointment. "How on earth did you get down here?"

Cameron finally relinquished his hold on the paint roller and dropped it at his feet. "Trevor climbed down and flipped a switch."

"He did what?" Terry asked, his eyes widening in shock.

"VIC told me to do it," Trevor said.

Terry folded his arms and glared at Trevor. "He did no such thing. Honestly, Trevor, there's a time and place for tomfoolery, but I'm afraid you've crossed the line."

"No, it's true," Nika said. "We all heard VIC give Trevor the instruction. It was the only way for us to get down here."

Terry's look of shock changed into one of perplexity as he turned his attention to Nika. "Were you riding in the cart when it crashed?"

Nika nodded, her eyes welling up with tears.

"Oh dear. May I?" Terry crossed the room, holding out his hands.

Nika sat back down in her chair while Terry began to examine her shoulders and arms. "I'm sorry," she said, sniffling. "I tried to be careful."

Trevor watched in bewilderment as Terry softly ran his fingers up and down Nika's neck.

"I think we're okay here," Terry whispered. "There doesn't appear to be any fracturing or swelling."

"But you don't know for sure, do you?" she whimpered.

"I'm not a doctor, no. But we have medical staff on hand for such an emergency. Your suit appears to have weathered the crash, though." Terry unzipped the pack on his belt and brought out a circular contraption with an extendable antenna. "If it's all right with you, this device will grant me access to your vitals, since your suit is not providing them." He attached the device to the top of Nika's helmet. After a few moments of silence, he removed the piece of equipment and returned it to his pack. "You have a slightly elevated heart rate, which is to be expected considering the circumstances, but had your body been experiencing any sort of serious distress, I would've seen a definite spike in your blood pressure." He placed his hand on Nika's shoulder and smiled. "I think you'll survive."

Cameron raised his hand. "Maybe you should inspect me too."

Terry glanced up from his examination, fixing Cameron with a concerned look. "Why? Are you in any pain?"

Cameron shifted his feet. "Well, no. I . . . I don't think so."

"Then I'm sure you're fine."

"But we were both riding in the same cart as Nika when it crashed," Devin said. "You're not going to at least check us?"

"Yeah, we could have internal injuries," Cameron added. "Maybe we're in shock."

"It wasn't that bad of an accident," Trevor said. "None of you were even thrown out."

"Well, why are you so concerned about Nika, then?" Devin asked. "Is it because she's a girl?"

Nika narrowed her eyes. "That's not the reason."

"Maybe we should make our way back to the observation deck," Terry said, turning to exit the room.

"I thought *that* was the exit." Devin pointed to the door behind the scaffolding.

Terry nodded at the wires dangling from the ceiling. "This whole area is still under heavy repair. We experienced some foundational cracking during the initial construction. You're likely to fall through the floor going that way, or get bombarded with crumbling drywall." It was at that moment that Terry noticed the lone helmet resting on the table. "Why did you take that off?" He glared at Trevor.

Trevor shrugged guiltily. "It wasn't working."

Terry picked up the helmet and examined the inside. "We were still collecting . . . It's unsafe not to have it on."

"That's what I tried to tell him," Cameron said. "But he didn't listen to me."

Terry angrily tossed the helmet aside. "This entire procedure has been an utter failure. You broke the cart, and now all of our research is basically for naught."

"I'll just put it back on." Trevor bent over to pick up the helmet, but Terry kicked it away from his reach. Trevor went after it, picked it up, and put it on hurriedly.

"There's no point now! Did you not hear what I said?"

"We didn't mean to break anything," Cameron said cautiously.

"Yeah, it was an accident," Nika added. "And it's not just Trevor's fault."

"I never said it was just Trevor's fault. You're all to blame." Terry stormed toward the open doorway, and Devin side-stepped out of his path. "And another thing"—he held up a gloved finger—"don't think for one minute that my brother will actually pay you for your services. As far as I'm concerned, this is an absolute breach of contract."

"Mr. Castleton!" Devin suddenly grabbed hold of Terry's arm and started pulling him away from the door.

"No payment. No reward. And no interviews! Let go of me!" Terry demanded.

But Devin wouldn't let go. And that's when Trevor realized there was something different about him. Devin looked a lot like he had when they were on the cart and he had insisted that they abort the ride. It wasn't just a change in how he spoke, but there also seemed to be an alteration to his physical appearance. His eyes looked deeper set, and his skin had turned an unhealthy shade of pale green. Devin clung to Terry's sleeve, heaving backward with all his weight.

"What's going on?" Trevor asked, but Devin wasn't given an opportunity to explain.

Just then, a pair of sharp claws on the end of two gangly green arms shot through the opening and wrapped around Terry's chest. In an instant, Mr. Castleton was gone.

"No!" Nika shouted, covering her visor with her hands. Cameron collapsed on the ground in shock. Even Trevor wasn't sure what to do and just stood next to the table frowning in disbelief.

"I . . . I tried to help him," Devin said, his voice trembling as he looked desperately at Trevor. He gaped at his fingertips, which only seconds before had gripped Terry's sleeve.

"Get over here, Devin," Trevor said firmly. At that moment, he could see the silhouettes of two shady figures racing for the door, their eyes gleaming like yellow spotlights.

Still trembling, Devin peered over his shoulder at the oncoming monsters. He tried to scream, but Trevor shoved him out of the way, forcing the air out of his lungs. Trevor pulled the door closed and locked the dead bolt as both creatures slammed headlong into it, sending a jarring wave through the metal. They squealed with rage as their claws dug into the door, trying to force their way in.

CHAPTER 24

THE CLAWING AND scratching lasted for only a few seconds, and then the sounds behind the door fell silent. Devin lay on the floor, his face buried in his hands. Why hadn't he acted more quickly? If he had just paid attention to his senses, he could've saved Mr. Castleton. Devin's eyes burned. If he wasn't careful, he would be crying in no time. Despite what his dad thought, seeing things right before they happened was rarely a blessing. In most cases, Devin's ability left him wondering if he could've done something more.

Squeezing his hands into fists, Devin sat up and tried to control his breathing. Trevor stood by the door, his ear pressed against the metal, listening.

"Please, get your hands off me," Nika said to Cameron,

who was practically hugging her. "I believe you're squeezing me too tightly."

Cameron released his hold on her arms and moved a step away. "I didn't know what else to do. Those creatures almost got us."

"They almost got *me*," Devin corrected. Although the creatures' true intentions seemed a little muddied to his mind. Devin didn't think they cared who they captured. Their only intent was to destroy.

"You said they were growing in pods," Cameron said to Devin. "How could they grow such things? You can't just bypass millions of years of evolution and create a new species!"

"Maybe they're actors dressed up in costume," Nika suggested.

"Oh right," Devin scoffed. "A bunch of actors who just hijacked the CEO's older brother. Safe to say those two bozos just cashed their last paychecks."

"No, they're definitely machines," Cameron said. "But they could be operating on a different system. Just because some components of the Adventure Machine have stopped doesn't mean all of them have."

Devin groaned. This was supposed to be the day of his arrival as an Internet star. First, he'd lost his dad's phone, which was probably smashed to bits at the bottom of the Globe along with hours of video footage. Then he'd failed to abort the adventure when he'd sensed danger. Then, he'd lost

Terry. Devin wondered if the others blamed him for not responding fast enough. He should be protecting them.

Trevor removed his ear from the door, then reached for the dead bolt. "I think they've left."

"Well, don't open the door!" Cameron gasped. "Even a complete idiot would know better than to do that."

"If I don't open the door, how are we going to help Mr. Castleton?" Trevor asked.

Cameron clenched his jaw. "Why do we have to help him? He wasn't being very nice."

Devin stood. "But I'm responsible for him. If I hadn't been so distracted, I could've done something."

"You couldn't have known what was going to happen," Nika said, scooting one of the chairs away from the table and easing herself down onto the seat.

Cameron removed his helmet, then his glasses, and breathed on them. "Technically, if anyone could have, it would've been Devin." He wiped the lenses on his sleeve, replaced them along with his helmet, and flinched when he noticed the three pairs of eyes glowering at him. "Why are you staring at me that way? I wasn't saying it was his fault, I'm just stating the facts. It's what I do."

"Yeah, well, I may not think before I do things, but you don't think before you speak," Trevor said. He eyed the door once more. "They couldn't have gone far. If we try to follow them, we might be able to talk some sense into the creatures."

Nika crossed her hands in her lap. "You really think that? They didn't seem interested in having a conversation."

"I got the feeling that they wanted to hurt us," Devin said. More than anything else. Not just hurt. Destroy. Eliminate. There was no arguing with the fact that the creatures' having kidnapped Mr. Castleton complicated things quite bit. Devin glanced over and noticed Cameron seated patiently in a chair with his hand raised. "Why are you raising your hand?"

"I'm following the suggestion of a person of lesser intelligence by thinking before I speak." Cameron's eyes shifted to each person in the room. Trevor raised an eyebrow. "I don't think we'll be of any help to Mr. Castleton by chasing them down," Cameron stated.

"Okay, Einstein, what do you suggest we do?" Devin asked. Cameron seemed to have an answer for everything, but there was no way Devin was just going to follow him blindly. There was book smarts and then there was common sense. And while Cameron had plenty of the first, he was severely lacking in the second. Devin would rather listen to Trevor's proposition, and that kid was borderline psychotic with his fearlessness. "We can't stay here. This room's a trap."

"No, no"—Cameron shook his head—"staying here is a terrible plan. I need my pills, and they're topside in my mom's purse. I already feel the placating effects of my last dosage starting to wear off, which is probably why I have such brilliant ideas at the moment, but things could get awkward here really soon if I don't get regulated."

"Are you going to babble, or do you actually have a suggestion?" Nika asked.

"Isn't it obvious?" Cameron danced his fingers across the large sheet of creased paper on the table.

"Can you even read that?" Trevor asked.

"I believe I have already made clear the magnitude of my IQ." Cameron jabbed his pointer finger on a spot near the corner of the blueprints. "That's us. We're in this room. Using these blueprints, we should be able to easily navigate our way out of this hole."

Nika leaned over the map as she followed Cameron's finger. "I thought you said you didn't want to go out there."

Cameron licked his lips. "Heavens no. I want to go that way." He gestured to the rear exit hidden behind the scaffolding. "I'd rather take my chances dodging a few falling ceiling tiles than risk getting eaten by those monsters."

"They're not going to eat us," Trevor groaned. "And your helmet is smoking, by the way."

Cameron nodded. "Precisely. My helmet is . . . My helmet is what?" He apprehensively cocked his head to one side.

Devin could see thin tendrils of smoke drifting up from the back of Cameron's, and Nika's heads. Panicked, he quickly disconnected his own helmet from his suit and tossed it aside. Nika did the same, in a calmer, more delicate manner. Trevor also followed suit, just in case. But Cameron was flailing about, squealing for help, and coughing violently. Trevor grabbed hold of Cameron's arms to stop him from thrashing, and undid his helmet. More vapor poured out, punctuated by several bright sparks from beneath the padding.

"This is horrible!" Cameron breathed. "We're trapped in this cramped room, without our helmets, and have no way to communicate with headquarters. And there are monsters all around us. We're going to die!"

Nika slapped Cameron across his cheek. It wasn't hard enough to dislodge his glasses from his nose, but the blow caused Cameron to turn his head sharply to one side.

"I shouldn't have done that," Nika said, staring worriedly down at her hand. She wiggled her fingers.

"*You* hit *me*." Cameron caressed his cheek where a light pink handprint had started to form.

"I slapped you," Nika corrected.

"What's the difference?"

"Where I come from, when someone starts to act out-of-control and unreasonable, we slap them."

"Well, where I come from, when someone acts the way I did, we just give them their pills."

"*Dedushka* was right," Nika muttered. "They can't keep me safe on this ride. I've endangered myself, and I have no control over my actions."

"What are you talking about?" Devin asked. Nika's eyes had zoned out. She stared past her flexing fingers, her lips quivering as if she was on the verge of tears. "Hello? Are you finished?" Devin tugged on the corner of the blueprints. "We're not getting anywhere."

Nika stiffened, lowering her hand and setting her jaw in determination. "My vote is to wait here. My grandfather will be along soon to get me, and he wouldn't approve of me taking any more risks."

Trevor shook his head. "Our parents think Terry is bringing us back. And he's too busy being . . ."

"Eaten," Cameron chimed in.

"Stop it," Trevor said. "I wasn't going to say that. It could take all day before they realize we're still down here. And then they'll have to suit up and walk all those miles of track."

"But what if more of those creatures are waiting for us outside?" Devin asked. "What if they . . ."

Something heavy pounded against the door, echoing through the small room. One after another, the creatures struck, rattling the walls, and toppling empty paint cans onto the floor.

"They must have brought some sort of battering ram," Cameron said breathlessly. "Because of course they would."

"I think we should leave. Now," Trevor suggested.

There was no further argument. The four of them hurriedly exited through the rear of the room.

CHAPTER 25

THE AIR WAS thick with dust. Nika could smell the strong scent of mildewed drywall and old paint. She wondered how Trevor managed to find his way along the path without clear vision. One misstep, and he could fall through the floor. But Trevor never lacked confidence, moving through the narrow, crumbling hallway without any reluctance. *What would that be like?* Nika wondered. *To not show any sign of fear?* Because of her condition, Nika seemed to be afraid of everything. Simple movements could cause her injury.

The group moved slowly and methodically, forced to clamber single file between huge stacks of sheetrock and two-by-fours, and sidestep around vast pools of spilled paint and garbage.

After hiking for several minutes, they arrived at a point in the hallway where the ceiling had clearly caved in, leaving another mountain of rubble blocking their path. The pile towered almost all the way to the top of the hall, but it took Trevor only a minute to point out the best route to take. He climbed up and then over, and slid down a sheet of metal to the other side. The others followed after him, but Nika took her time. Regardless of how she envied Trevor's self-assurance, she refused to rush any of her steps until she felt confident that the pile would hold.

Though the noise was muffled by the pile of debris, Nika could hear the creatures still pounding against the door, grunting and howling in anger. They were getting louder, more persistent, and she knew the door wouldn't hold much longer.

"Dudes, you've got to keep walking," Devin said. He plowed into Nika for the third time as he looked over his shoulder.

"Please, stop running into me," Nika begged, pausing to run her fingers along her shoulders. "We're going as fast as we can." She knew Devin was just as worried as she was, but he could be so reckless. Of course he couldn't have known it, but just nudging Nika the wrong way could cause her injury.

"And might I point out that you volunteered to bring up the rear, Devin?" Cameron said.

"Sure. Point it out," Devin fired back. "But if those things start chasing us, I think you should probably know that I'm a much faster runner than you are."

Cameron trailed behind Trevor, his faced buried in the blueprints. "We should be seeing it now." He glanced up and tapped Trevor on the shoulder, pointing. "What did I tell you? There's the door to the stairwell." He tucked the blueprints into a folded square beneath his armpit. A grayish door stood less than twenty feet away. According to Cameron, they would find three flights of stairs and end up exiting through another door into the food court.

There was just one problem.

Trevor moved to one side to show the others a gigantic chasm spanning from wall to wall, lying between them and the door. The distance to the other side was at least twelve feet wide. Impossible to leap across without a running start. And even then, the ground looked too precarious to jump upon. More of the floor could give way.

"Oh dear." Cameron unfolded the blueprints once more and began searching for an alternate route. "There's no other way around it."

"We should've stayed in the room," Nika huffed. They didn't think things through. Mr. Castleton had warned them of the dangers lurking in the hallway. Now where were they to go? "We had plenty of objects to barricade ourselves until help could come."

Nika caught her breath in her throat as she felt the weakened tile crumbling beneath her weight. At first glance, the hole appeared to be bottomless, but as she strained her eyes, she eventually saw the thin, weaving outline of the Adventure Machine track several hundred feet below. The pounding from the other end of the hallway came to an abrupt conclusion, followed by the sound of scrabbling claws against the tile floor.

"They're through!" Devin hissed. "Might as well just throw ourselves down that hole now."

Trevor rubbed his eyes with his knuckles and stared at the ceiling. "What about that?" he suggested, pointing to where a single wire dangled down from one of the missing panels. Black insulated coating covered the wire, but the end had been frayed to where it now looked like a shoelace without the plastic tip.

"That could be live," Cameron warned. "It might shock us."

Nika could hear the steady hum of electricity coursing through the wire and she moved back a step.

Trevor never hesitated as he reached out and plucked the coppery end in his gloved hand. Nika gasped, cringing as she waited for the worst to happen. A sudden electrical jolt could send Trevor down the hole. He tugged sharply to test its strength, but it didn't give way. Dropping to his knees, Trevor applied his full weight. The wire continued to hold.

"This suit keeps us from getting zapped." Trevor rolled the frayed tip between his thumb and forefinger. "And the wire's strong."

"I've never done any rope swinging before," Nika said.

"There's no better time to try it out." Trevor wrapped the end of the wire around his left forearm and reached farther up with his free hand. Then he took a step back and leapt. Above him, powdered pieces of drywall showered down, and something groaned in the ceiling, as though the strain of the weight might cause another roof collapse at any moment.

But the wire held.

As Trevor's feet connected with the tile on the other side, he kept hold for a moment to gain his balance. When he let go, the wire snapped back to its original position.

Cameron had to stand on his tippy-toes to reach and yelped when Devin shoved him across the gap. He held his breath as Trevor reached out and plucked him from the vine like a lightweight summer squash.

Devin went next and made it over without incident.

"It's like *Pitfall!*" Devin said as Trevor grasped him around his waist and guided him to a safe spot on the floor.

"Is that another movie?" Trevor asked.

"It's an old video game. Only in *Pitfall!* there are alligators snapping at you as you swing across." Devin peered down into the hole. "My dad has an Atari 2600 he keeps in the basement and I sneak down and play it every now and then when he works late."

"I can't do this. I'll fall, or . . ." Nika hesitated, shrinking away from the wire. There were too many dangers involved. She had already risked too much. First it was the pressure on the ride, and then she endured the crash. Nika knew she shouldn't tempt fate anymore. Her luck was destined to run out. "Can you see if there's something you could lay across the hole? It has to be solid. Something I could crawl over."

Trevor and Devin scanned the area for what they could find, but aside from a few straggling pieces of lumber, nothing seemed sturdy or long enough to use as a bridge.

"It's easy," Cameron said to Nika. "If I can do it, you should have no problem."

"You don't understand. None of you do." Nika closed her trembling fingers around the wire. "What if I slip?"

"Not to rush you," Trevor said evenly. "But you may want to hurry it up a little."

"Why?" She jerked her head around and noticed several large pieces of rock topple down from the collapsed mound of debris at the far end of the hallway.

One of the creatures poked its head out from the opening at the top of the pile and then slid down the slide to the floor. Nika panted a few rapid breaths, twisted the wire tightly in her hands, and leapt off the edge.

Had she decided to jump before the others, she might have made it across the hole to safety. But the strain of having to support the weight of the three boys proved to be too much, and the wire produced a sickening pop as it dropped several feet more from the ceiling, sending Nika down into the hole.

CHAPTER 26

NIKA EXPELLED A loud burst of air from the impact of hitting the side wall's concrete, and her hands slipped from the wire. She desperately lunged for the edge of the hole and grasped the crumbling rock with her fingers.

"Hang on!" Devin shouted. With Trevor holding on to the back of his neotanium suit, Devin bent down into the hole and pulled Nika up by her arms. She dug her fingers into his wrists, but she wasn't breathing.

"What's wrong with her?" Cameron demanded, hopping from one foot to the other. "Why is her face that color?"

"I think she just got the wind knocked out of her," Trevor said.

Nika finally released a breath and began sobbing

immediately. Despite how amazing the neotanium suit had been in protecting her on the ride, nothing could have withstood that blow. Nika knew she was in trouble. The injuries would be severe, but she didn't have time to dwell on them.

"Cameron, look out!" she warned as the first creature leapt across the gap and landed effortlessly a few feet away.

Cameron froze in place, a tiny statue, staring up at the imposing monster.

"We don't want any trouble," Trevor said, stepping in front of Cameron and holding his hands out in a nonthreatening gesture. He tried shoving Cameron away, but the small boy seemed to have sprouted roots. "Get to the door," Trevor urged.

"I . . . can't." Cameron's small voice seemed to come from somewhere other than his mouth, buried deep in his throat.

"Move."

Nika watched in horror as the creature's trapezoidal head twitched, its eyes homing in on its closest target. Trevor.

"We're just going to leave, okay? Slow and easy." Trevor stepped backward, his heel nudging Cameron's foot.

"Hurry up!" Devin shouted from the doorway.

The sound of Devin's voice must have triggered something, because the creature suddenly lashed out, seizing hold of Trevor's collar. Its eyes tapered into slits as it hoisted him high above its head.

"It's going to throw him in!" Devin shouted. "I can see it!"

Nika couldn't believe this was happening. What was Doug Castleton doing at that moment? Could he see what was going on, but was powerless to stop it?

"Help us! Please!" Nika screamed. "You've got to do something!"

"Come *on*." Trevor locked his fingers around the creature's wrist. "You don't have to do this." He struggled against its powerful grip and stared down into the hole.

Nika wanted to jump to her feet and help Trevor, but all her strength had vanished the moment she collapsed into the wall. "What do we do, Devin?" She looked pleadingly up at him and noticed a strange smile on Devin's lips. "Why are you smiling?" she demanded.

"Look!" Devin pointed, and Nika watched as the creature's eyes widened to the size of golf balls.

"How does that taste?" Cameron screamed from below the monster, jabbing the live electrical wire into its side. "Hmmm? Want some more?" He poked the wire into its arm, and it dropped Trevor to the floor.

"Yeah!" Devin cheered from the doorway, pumping his fist. "Go, Cameron!"

Shrieking in agony, the creature tried to shield itself, but Cameron zapped it again, the frayed copper end of the wire connecting with its palm.

Cameron grinned at Trevor. "This is fun."

"Hey, watch what you're doing!" Trevor warned, leaping to his feet.

"Take that!" Cameron wasn't listening. "And that, and that, and that," he chanted, each "that" underscored by another jolt of his wire.

The second creature had made it down the metal slide, slipping and skidding across the tile. It covered the distance in a matter of seconds, then leapt to the other side and closed its claws around Cameron's shoulders. Cameron turned and continued to zap, unleashing a barrage of strikes, impossible to block. Before anyone else could react, both creatures were toppling over the edge and falling into the hole.

CHAPTER 27

WITH THE CREATURES no longer a threat, a hollow pit formed in Nika's stomach. Why had she listened to the others? Why had she tried to swing across the hole? She wanted to scream at the top of her lungs, but by the way her body shook, she doubted she possessed the strength to even utter a whimper.

"Are you going to stand up, or what?" Devin asked her. He had managed to slide Nika toward the stairwell door and had it propped open with his leg.

Nika could feel Devin gawking at her, though she kept her eyes fixed on the ceiling. He didn't understand. In Devin's mind, in Trevor's, everything was great. They had survived an attack by the creatures, and now they would be reunited with their parents. The horrible day was over for them, they would go back to their normal lives and have an exciting story to tell their friends about the adventure. But not Nika. Never in her life had she experienced a fall like that. An impact half as harsh could've crushed every bone in her body. It was a miracle she had managed to keep hold on the wire and not plummet to her death.

"I was in a zone, I believe. That's the only explanation," Cameron blabbered. "I must have crossed over to a higher plane of hyperactivity. It's all a dizzying blur." Nika lowered her eyes and watched as Trevor and Cameron approached. Nothing seemed capable of erasing the grin chiseled permanently on Cameron's lips. "I didn't even have to declothe. Progress." Cameron tugged on Trevor's sleeve. "And I saved your life. We're bonded to each other forever."

"What's wrong with her?" Trevor asked, looking at Nika.

"You got me," Devin said.

Nika blinked, sending a stream of tears cascading down her cheeks. Her lips trembled, but she didn't speak.

Trevor squatted beside Nika and snapped his fingers next to her ears. "Can you hear me?"

"I'm injured," she answered, in a voice barely louder than a whisper.

"Where does it hurt?" Trevor asked.

"She doesn't feel pain, remember?" Cameron said. "It's her congenital insensitivity."

Devin sucked back on his teeth and looked at Trevor. "That's a bummer."

"You did hit pretty hard, but they can give you some medicine or something upstairs," Trevor reasoned.

Nika made a slight movement with her head, shaking it back and forth only an inch. "It's worse than that."

"There's something else you're not telling us, isn't there?" Cameron asked.

How could she tell them? Now they would know all about her. How weak and broken and different she was from everyone else. They would never treat her the same. But she had to tell them. Her health was more important than her pride. "Congenital insensitivity isn't the only condition I have," she said, taking a deep breath and pausing before she continued. "I've also been diagnosed with a rare form of osteogenesis imperfecta."

Trevor and Devin looked at each other with befuddled expressions.

"Oh dear." Cameron pressed his fingertips together under his chin and sighed. "This is not good."

"You know what she's talking about?" Trevor asked him.

"It means her bones are weaker than a normal person's," Cameron explained, staring down at Nika as though she were some specimen in a lab. "She's more susceptible to injuries."

"So, how bad is it?" Trevor asked.

"After a fall like that," Cameron said. "She could have multiple broken ribs, punctured lungs, internal bleeding."

"Seriously?" Devin looked skeptical. "You barely bounced off the wall."

"Brittle bone disease and congenital insensitivity? Talk about a double whammy," Cameron said, clucking. "You probably should've never been allowed on the Adventure Machine."

Nika wanted to explode with anger. To leap to her feet, shake Cameron by his shoulders, and wipe that smug, condescending look from his face. But she couldn't do that, because he was right. She never should have convinced her grandfather to let her leave Chelyabinsk. "It's true," Nika whimpered, sucking in a shuddering breath. "I need to be stabilized, and I need my doctor. I have no way of knowing how bad my injuries are without X-rays."

"I could go up alone and bring someone back," Trevor offered.

"By yourself?" Devin asked.

In an instant, Cameron's curious smile disappeared. "Yeah, by yourself?"

"One of you could come with me, I guess," Trevor suggested. "While the other could stay with her."

"I don't want to stay down here." Cameron slid in close to Trevor as if he was about to latch onto his leg.

"Me either," Devin said. "No offense, Nika."

"Then just leave me. All of you. I'll be fine. I don't want anyone to have to do something they're not comfortable with." There was no point in making them all suffer along with her. It wasn't like they were really her friends anyways. No one stayed friends with Nika for very long. Not after they discovered the true nature of her condition.

"What if we carried you up the stairs?" Trevor asked. "We would be really careful not to bump into anything."

Nika scrunched her eyebrows in thought. "It'll just slow you down."

"So?" Trevor said. "We're not just going to leave you here with those other creatures hanging around."

"How many more are there?" Cameron asked.

"I counted six pods the other night," Trevor said.

"Which means we have four left to worry about." Cameron winked at Trevor. "Thanks to me."

"You might cause more injuries," Nika said. "I'd have no way to prevent myself from falling."

"How about you walk on your own, then. But we'll support you like this"—Cameron put his arm over Trevor's shoulders to show her his plan—"like soldiers do when one of them is wounded on the battlefield."

"You really want to help me?" Nika asked. "Even you?" She looked at Devin.

Devin looked stunned. "Even me? Oh, because I'm a big jerk, right?"

"No, that's not it. You have been friendly. It is I who held back. About my conditions. About everything." Nika pursed her lips, then extended a hand out to Devin. "As long as we go slow, I'm willing to try."

Chapter 28

THE GROUP HIKED the first couple of flights, with Devin and Trevor shouldering the bulk of the burden. Nika didn't weigh much, but she was too worried to put much weight on her legs, forcing the boys to support her most of the distance. The pleasantly pungent aroma of what smelled like cooked garlic seeped through the walls, permeating the stairwell. Devin breathed in the scent, his stomach tightening with anticipation. He hadn't thought much about food once they started their adventure, but now that he could smell it, he realized that it had been almost five hours since breakfast.

"Can you smell that?" Trevor asked. "I bet that's lunch."

"So what's going to happen to you now?" Devin asked Nika.

"What do you mean?" She slowed, gripping Devin and Trevor's suits with her fingers for balance.

"Well, what will your grandfather do when he finds out what happened?"

Nika swallowed. "It won't be good. He's very protective of me. I have never been permitted to do much. These injuries will certainly make life more difficult."

"It's not your fault you fell," Trevor said. "If you think about it, if you didn't try to swing across the hole, you would've eventually been grabbed by those creatures. One way or another you were headed for an accident. Your grandfather should be happy you jumped."

Nika smiled, but then grimaced. "That's not how my grandfather operates. He finds very little good in accidents. He will blame the Castletons, the Adventure Machine, all of California. He would never blame me outright, but I will be punished just the same. My activities will be restricted more heavily. I won't be allowed to go outside for months."

"Say something to him, then," Devin said. "Tell him it's not cool to treat you like some breakable doll. It's your life, you know?" Devin felt sorry for Nika. Of the four of them, she had the most difficult life.

Nika came to a stop. "Say something to my grandfather? It's not that simple."

"Sure it is," Devin said.

"Oh really? Then why haven't you stood up to your father?" she asked.

Devin flinched. "What's my father have anything to do with this?"

"He's ruling your life with his camera," Nika said. "He's forcing you to act a certain way. To behave differently in order to someday become famous. And you're not happy about it."

Devin opened his mouth to argue, but Trevor cut him off.

"She's got you on that, dude," Trevor said. "You said earlier about how you don't really want to be on YouTube. Sounds to me like you should be saying something to him too."

"Agreed," Cameron added, his face still buried in the blueprints. "If your recommendation to Nika is to stand up to her grandfather, you should do the same yourself with your father. Otherwise, your words have no bearing."

Devin frowned. Why were they all of a sudden turning on him? "Look, it's not like either one of us is going to do anything about it. So let's just drop it."

Beyond the exit, the familiar lights of Bortho's Burgers and Beets & Weeds from the food court poured through the opening. The trickling sound of water from the fountains was a welcome change from the silence inside the Globe. Several banquet tables had been laid out at the center of the food court, brimming with food. Devin and Trevor carried

Nika the rest of the way and gently lowered her into a chair next to one of the fountains.

"It says we're supposed to go ahead and eat." Cameron held up a note he plucked from a table and handed the folded piece of paper to Devin to read.

> *Hope you had a great adventure,*
> *my friends. We'll be along shortly.*
> *Help yourselves to lunch.*
>
> > *Doug*

Devin tossed the note aside and grabbed a warm plate from the stack next to the first covered chafing dish. There were ten platters in all, each containing a different delicacy. Fried chicken legs, enchilada soup with tortilla strips and sour cream, and buttery corn on the cob, so plump, the kernels looked on the verge of popping. Devin discovered the source of the garlicky smell inside the fourth chafing dish: seasoned whipped potatoes with creamy, peppery gravy. He ladled a mountainous spoonful of the potatoes onto his plate and plopped a juicy pork chop across the mound. Cameron and Trevor stacked their plates as well, each of them discovering at least one of their favorite meals among the selections.

"I didn't realize how hungry I was until I saw all this

food," Devin said, opening a cooler beneath the last table and grabbing two cans of cold soda from the cubes of ice.

"Don't you think it's a little strange how Doug somehow knew we would be here?" Nika asked, snapping Devin from his food trance. He had just bitten into a chicken leg, his eyes closed in satisfaction. "He left us a note, but why wouldn't our guardians be here as well?"

"Strange?" Devin popped open one of the sodas and dark brown fizz bubbled out from the lid. "Maybe. But no point in letting this good food go to waste."

"Well, I don't like it. This whole setup seems odd to me. And aren't you forgetting something?" She looked expectantly at Trevor. "I want to go to the on-site clinic and see the doctor right away."

Trevor was working his way through the final third of a rib eye steak. He wiped his chin with the back of his hand. "Your grandfather will be along with the others, won't he? Maybe we should wait for them."

Nika gingerly pressed her hands against the table and slid her seat out from under it. "Are you not going to help me?"

Suddenly, Cameron bolted out of his chair, holding his finger to his ear. "Can you hear that?"

Devin sat still to listen, but all he could hear was Trevor chomping noisily on a slab of meat too big for his mouth.

"Stop that." Cameron pointed at Trevor. "Listen!"

Trevor reluctantly stopped chewing.

And that's when they all heard it, faint and distant, and almost completely masked by the burbling fountains in the food court. The sound of someone crying.

Not just crying. Bawling.

The owner of the voice wailed and sobbed and howled and blubbered. And in between each burst of weeping, Trevor heard a loud chopping noise.

Thwack!

Devin swallowed and nodded toward Samurai Sal's, the next booth down from Bortho's. "It's coming from there."

The wailing grew louder by the moment, interspersed with the sharp, rhythmic thwacks, which also seemed to be increasing in volume. The sushi restaurant appeared to be closed. All the lights had been turned off with the exception of a single bulb shining behind the counter. But standing in the preparation kitchen, sobbing and chopping the frozen head of a steely-eyed fish with her meat cleaver, was none other than Shrill Parker.

CHAPTER 29

SHRILL STILL WORE the same horror outfit from earlier, but her makeup looked streaked and splotchy, no doubt the result of all her crying. Cameron tensed. He had hoped never again to cross paths with the disturbed actress. Her little stunt earlier in the elevator had nearly caused Cameron to have an accident.

Thwack!

The cleaver came down solidly on the frozen fish skull, spraying bits of scale and frost into the air.

Cameron desperately tugged on Trevor's sleeve, his eyes rapidly switching between Trevor and the Butcher's Bride. "We need to leave," he urged.

This was not acceptable. Shrill Parker was the last person

Cameron expected to see in the food court. A sobbing psychopathic murderer, even one who only acted as such in movies, was not to be trifled with. Cameron eyed Shrill's cleaver, now covered in gooey fish parts. The weapon was larger than any of his mother's knives back home in their kitchen. And what Shrill was doing to that poor fish made no culinary sense. She might as well have plopped it into a blender and pressed frappé.

Thwack!

Shrill embedded the blade into the fish, then wiggled and strained to remove it.

"Ms. Parker?" Trevor asked. "Is everything all right?"

Thwack!

Another outburst of sobbing.

"Ms. Parker?" Trevor repeated.

This time, Shrill sniffled, and paused mid-chop, lowering the cleaver. "I'm sorry. I was just . . . just . . ." She blinked, recognition dawning in her eyes as a slight smile appeared on her lips. "Oh, it's you. Aren't you supposed to be testing the Adventure Machine right now?"

"We are. I mean, we were." Trevor averted his eyes to the head of the decapitated fish lying on the counter.

"How was the ride?" Shrill asked. "Did it thrill you?"

Nika wrapped her arms around herself. "Not exactly. The ride actually broke down."

Shrill curled her lower lip incredulously, but then her

eyebrows twitched as the faint smile on her lips stretched into a full grin. "That has to be the single most amazing piece of news I have heard in quite some time."

"Huh?" Devin blurted.

Shrill laughed. "Serves them right. All of them!"

"Who are you talking about?" Devin asked.

"Who do you think?" she fired back, suddenly harsh. "The Castletons, of course. And all those associated with this horrible, horrible attraction."

Trevor scratched the back of his neck. "Aren't you a part of the Adventure Machine?"

"Was," Shrill corrected him, her voice firm. "I *was* a part of the Adventure Machine, up until earlier, when you and your parents reacted so savagely to my performance. Doug fired me. Decided I was no longer the right fit for the project. That if I caused that sort of response, I would frighten away thousands of potential customers. They threw me out like some washed-up has-been." She raised the cleaver and stared at her reflection in the blade. "And I suppose I have you little lovelies to thank for that."

"Thank us?" Trevor asked. "What's that supposed to mean?"

"Textbook behavior!" Cameron blurted. "She's displaying the textbook behavior of someone with devious intentions."

Trevor cracked a smile. "What are you trying to say?"

Cameron groaned. "Isn't it obvious?" Cameron liked

Trevor, truly he did. But the boy could be so daft at times. All of them were the same. Why couldn't they see the writing on the wall? From Cameron's extensive research in psychology, he knew what Shrill Parker was about to do.

"I hope you brought your bibs," Shrill said. "Because it's about to get messy in here." She unleashed an impressive cackle, which echoed throughout the food court.

"Go, Trevor, go!" Nika urged, yanking on his arm. Though she still leaned against Trevor's body for support, Nika pulled him away from the restaurant as Shrill reached Samurai Sal's checkout counter and began climbing over.

The whooshing sound of her cleaver sliced through the air. It hadn't come close enough to strike any of them, but Cameron felt the breeze from the blade, and he gasped in disbelief.

"Won't you stay around so I can properly show you my appreciation?" Shrill expertly twirled the weapon in between her fingers.

Despite Cameron's height disadvantage, he kept pace with Devin as they turned and raced toward the lobby. They arrived at the elevators behind the hotel check-in desk, with Nika and Trevor close behind.

"What's wrong with this stupid thing?" Devin growled, repeatedly mashing the call button with his thumb.

"Where are our parents?" Cameron demanded. "They should be here. There are cameras everywhere!" He waved his hands frantically at one of the infrared eyes peering down at him from the ceiling. The red light above the camera blipped. "Hello?" he screamed. "I need my pills. I want to go home! And don't you hit me!" Cameron pointed a warning finger at Nika.

"I'm not going to hit you. But where do you plan on going?" she asked Devin, her voice frantic.

"I'm going to my hotel room, and then I'm calling the police. If this stupid elevator would ever hurry up."

"There has to be a phone somewhere down here," Trevor said. "They would have one at the receptionist's desk."

"Oh, for sure there is." Devin smacked the wall while keeping a constant eye on the Gallery behind them. He added a kick for good measure. "But that's back that way, and I'm not going anywhere near that psychopath."

"Oh, my little daaarlings!" Shrill stood in the entryway of the Gallery on the other side of the lobby, the cleaver dangling loosely at her side.

Cameron dug his knuckle into the call button, and pressed his ear against the door to listen. "I can hear it moving; at least, I think that's what I'm hearing."

The door remained closed as a robotic voice announced that the elevator was out of order.

"Out of order?" Devin cried. "This whole place is the worst!"

"Ah, ah, ah," Shrill's high-pitched voice squealed from a

lot closer. Cameron looked back just in time to see her chopping a wedge of the wall off with her cleaver. "Looks like you have no other place to go."

There *was* no way around her. The crazy woman had expertly blocked any chance of escape, and with the elevator broken, like everything else at the facility, Cameron and his friends were trapped. Digging his fingers in the corners of his eyes, Cameron tried to make sense of it all. She was just an actor. Someone paid to frighten them. That was all! The whole scenario seemed fishy, and not just because Shrill had spent the last few minutes hacking at seafood. Cameron desperately tugged on Trevor's sleeve.

"Can't you do something?" Cameron pleaded.

"Do what?" Trevor asked.

"Go over there and talk some sense into her. You're not afraid of anything!"

Trevor laughed. "Yeah, but I don't think she's going to listen to me."

A section of the wall to the side of the elevators suddenly started moving. Cameron blinked, thinking his eyes were playing tricks on him. The entire section collapsed inward as a dark entryway materialized in the wall.

"Hey, guys?" Cameron turned to the others to determine whether they were seeing the same thing.

A heavyset man wearing a sloppy, food-stained lab coat stood in the opening. The man's eyes were wide and worried, and when he noticed Cameron staring at him from across the way, he waved, urging Cameron to join him. "Yes, yes! Come on!" The man nodded vigorously, his voice booming as he beckoned. The sound was so loud, it startled Shrill in mid-cackle. The rest of the kids momentarily broke focus with the scream queen, their faces contorting with confusion.

"Where did he come from?" Nika wondered.

"Should we go to him?" Cameron asked.

Grabbing Cameron by the back of his collar, Trevor didn't pause long enough to answer as he led the three of them over to the door.

"Where do you think you're going?" Shrill screamed, her temporary trance broken. Then she chucked her meat cleaver at the children. It flew end over end and stuck into the wall as they rushed through the opening and the door to the secret passage sealed behind them.

CHAPTER 30

WITH THE DOOR closed and no light to speak of, it took Trevor a few moments before his eyes adjusted to the darkness. Soon he could make out the outline of Devin, Nika, and Cameron standing close by.

"That woman's going to jail!" Devin barked. "You can't chase kids with a hatchet. Wait until my dad finds out about it."

Trevor could hear the fumbling sounds of someone unfamiliar with the layout of the room searching for a light switch. "It's gotta be around here somewhere," the man grumbled through uneven breaths. He slapped the wall, expelling oofs and grunts as he stumbled over unseen obstacles. "Found it!" He tugged on a string, and a single bulb flickered on overhead.

Suddenly, Nika unleashed an earsplitting shriek. She covered her mouth with her hand, but it barely muffled the sound. A creature like the one that had chased them through the Globe stood a few feet away, towering above the heavyset man at the center of the room.

"It's okay!" The man stepped in front of the creature. "He's not going to hurt you."

"Yeah, right! Just like he didn't hurt Mr. Castleton, huh?" Devin pressed his back against the far wall, but there was no place for him to hide. The room wasn't much bigger than a large walk-in closet. A single computer monitor sat atop a thin desk, and five leather chairs on rolling casters rested in front of the monitor.

"Please, do not be alarmed," the creature said.

"It talks?" Devin dragged his hands down the sides of his helmet.

"Typically, they have their own form of communication. That's how I programmed them," the man said.

"Who are you?" Nika asked.

"Oh, sorry." The man wiped his hands on his lab coat. "My name's Harold Dippetts. I'm the head architect for the Adventure Machine. I wanted to be introduced to the four of you prior to your launch, but that didn't work out, so . . . here I am."

"Okay," Devin said. "Why are you hanging out with that thing?"

"Who? One here?" Harold glanced over his shoulder and pointed at the creature. "That's just how this worked out. I couldn't control every detail. Had to work rapidly to upload the glitch into the system."

Great! Trevor thought. Just what they needed. Another Cameron. Why couldn't these types realize how impossible it was for others to understand them? "Wait a minute. You're One?" Trevor asked.

The creature nodded, and a thin smile, hardly noticeable, broke across his face. "Yes, and we've met twice before, Trevor Isaacs. You might consider us as old friends."

Cameron removed his glasses and breathed on the lenses. "Old friends? I highly doubt that. You tried to kill us!"

One closed his eyes and bowed apologetically. "Oh no. I had nothing to do with the attack. That was Three and Five. They were unfortunate mishaps and had to be decommissioned."

"Decommissioned?" Cameron scoffed. "You mean destroyed." Then he brightened. "Thanks to me."

"Right. We get it," Trevor groaned. Enough was enough already.

"So why did your buddies attack us?" Devin asked. "We didn't do anything to them."

"They are creatures bound by very particular coding," One explained, his voice rhythmic and smooth, like the gentle hum of an oscillating fan. "You can't blame them for what they've been programmed to do."

"Er . . . excuse me, kids," Harold interrupted. "This is just a glitch, and we don't have much time. There are things we need to discuss before I let you back at it. I tried to tell you when you first exited the cart, but my hack failed, and Igrot's message was cut short and probably didn't make any sense."

Trevor stared at the others and then scrunched his forehead. "Who?"

"Igrot," Harold said, scanning the room of confused faces. "Igrot the Slime? You don't know who I'm talking about? Seriously? It was a really popular television show back in the eighties. Well, popular for about three or four episodes. They cancelled it after only one season. Such a shame. Brilliant story."

"Mr. . . . Harold, was it?" Cameron chimed in. "We've had a very long day."

Harold flipped his hand dismissively. "Igrot and his gang were a breed of advanced troglodyte warriors." He bobbed his head up and down, as if that would clarify everything. "You know. Lizard men."

"Lizard men?" A light suddenly went on in Trevor's mind. "You sent that lizard guy back in the cave?"

"Uh-huh. It was a nightmare trying to sneak in that upload. As was this." He held out his hand gesturing to the walls.

"But like I said before, the message was cut short, as this one will be unless we hurry. Please, all of you, sit down." Harold nodded to the row of chairs.

Once they were seated, One moved and stood, sentry-like, in front of the door, and Harold turned on the monitor. "By now, you've probably figured out there was no real contest. I mean, it was real, publicized, paid for, and all that. But the results were rigged."

"To get us here because of our abilities," Nika said.

"Bingo!" Harold snapped his fingers.

"But why?" Devin asked. "Why did they have to trick us and our parents into coming here? I would've come regardless."

"What did Igrot tell you?" Harold asked.

"He said we were being stolen," Trevor said. "Which really didn't make any sense."

"You? No. Your abilities, on the other hand, yes. Well, *replicated* is a better word for it." Harold nodded at the creature standing at the door. "The Adventure Machine is siphoning your abilities and putting them into One."

"Into One?" Trevor frowned. "What does that mean?"

Harold reclined in his seat and swiveled to face the creature. "One, how is it you're able to talk? I didn't initially program you to do that."

One tilted his head to the side, studying Harold with

interest, before pointing across the room. "I suppose he taught me."

"Me?" Cameron's voice cracked.

One nodded. "I've been designed to rapidly glean information from live human test subjects. My intellect has increased because of Cameron, thus my aptitude for speech and ingenuity."

"And him." Harold pointed at Devin. "What about him?"

"I gained superb anticipation abilities from Devin. I can now foresee events before they take place. I understand patterns and movement, and my mind clears when necessary to anticipate reaction."

"Sound familiar?" Harold asked Devin.

Devin shrugged, staring at One apprehensively.

"Because of you, Trevor, I have no sensation of fear." One pressed his hand against his chest and closed his eyes. "I find it invigorating."

"I was given an assignment to create an entity to fulfill a purpose on the Adventure Machine," Harold said, smearing the sweat from his cheek with his hand and wiping it on his already-filthy lab coat. "A final upload was required to complete the program, and we needed you four to finish our creation. One is now the most highly advanced artificially intelligent being in existence. Thanks to you."

"You're welcome," Trevor said.

Harold shook his head vehemently. "That was just a figure of speech. What I should have said was, thanks to you, we've created the most highly advanced artificially intelligent *weapon* in existence."

"Weapon?" Devin asked. "But it's just a theme park attraction."

"That's what I thought," Harold said. "I was hired under the impression that the creatures were to enhance the riders' experience. Give them a true taste of fear and excitement. You've been hunted by them. Didn't they scare you?"

Nika, Cameron, and Devin all nodded. Trevor just sat there listlessly.

"Well, not you, of course," Harold said, swatting a hand at Trevor. "But it's supposed to be fun, huh? An adventure. A thrill. Boy, was I ever wrong." The black monitor screen fizzed as an image appeared, revealing a photograph. Trevor squinted as he stared at the picture of a man with shiny, dark hair, and wearing a detestable grin.

"Recognize this man?" Harold asked.

"Yes, I do," Nika said. "It's the lawyer from earlier. Mr. Crones."

Harold chuckled. "That's just what he wants you to think, but that's not his real name. And believe me, he's no lawyer."

"You mean he's not a lawyer in the traditional sense," Cameron said. "He's more of a representative for the California Theme Park Approval Board."

"Nope. I mean he's no more a lawyer than I'm a hunky fitness model." Harold jabbed a thumb at his jiggling belly. "Mr. Crones is actually Howard Dimwalls, and he is a sneaky, conniving man. Wealthy, powerful, and hungry for one thing and one thing only."

"Which is?" Nika asked.

"Absolute wealth and absolute power!" Harold stamped his foot. "He's like an evil weapons dealer, only instead of guns and missiles and ammo, Dimwalls deals in stolen information, and the Adventure Machine technology is the missing piece he needs."

"How do you know all this?" Devin asked.

"Because I used to work for him," Harold said. "Years ago, when I was just a young programmer. I was a lot thinner then, and more naive. Dimwalls has been trying to manipulate artificially intelligent software for decades. He wants to use it to steal information and ideas and whatever else he can get his grubby hands on."

"Maybe you've got the wrong guy," Trevor suggested. "The Castletons think he's legit."

Harold raised an eyebrow. "Do they?" He pointed at the screen as the image of Mr. Dimwalls changed into one of a typed message. "This is an email I intercepted that was sent to Mr. Dimwalls from this facility, promising to sell the Adventure Machine technology to him for an undisclosed amount of money. I don't know exactly who sent it either, because they did a good job encrypting that part of the email, despite all my efforts to decode it. But I do know that it came from the tenth floor."

"So?" Trevor asked.

Harold blinked. "Well, that's where all the important people meet. The executives. And at the time I intercepted it, there were only two individuals on that floor. Doug and Terry Castleton. I know because Terry drives a Volvo and Doug drives some freakishly fast monstrosity that might as well have wings."

"How is it you were able to intercept this email?" Cameron asked. "With something that secret, you would think they would have been more cautious."

Harold sighed. "Howard Dimwalls. Harold Dippetts. My guess is they were so nervous at the time trying to set up the deal, they didn't even think to double-check the email address."

"Okay, hold on," Trevor said. "Even if this Dimwalls guy is some no-good criminal, what good would a roller coaster do to someone dealing with information?"

"The technology we've created collects your ideas, and feeds on your intellect."

"That's how the ride knew to produce the moose. My worst fear!"

"Exactly!" Harold glanced down at his wristwatch for the tenth time. "Can you imagine what would happen if that technology fell into the wrong hands? Someone could pioneer a way to steal everyone's ideas. They could discover dangerous secrets. A program like that could wipe out any company from just pirating their information. It could cripple entire countries!"

Nika rubbed her eyes. "Why are you telling us this?"

"Because I need your help to put a stop to it," Harold explained.

"Us?" Cameron straightened in his seat. "If you knew all along about this secret dealing between the Castletons and Mr. Dimwalls, why didn't you go to the police?"

Harold's shoulders slumped. "What am I supposed to do? March up to the tenth floor, without an appointment, knock on Doug's door and say, 'Hey, chuckles, someone's trying to sell dangerous technology to a well-known criminal, and by golly, I think it's you'?"

Trevor laughed. "I would pay to watch you do that."

"And I can't stop this from happening from the outside," Harold continued. "The technology is too deeply rooted. What are the police going to do with something no one has ever encountered? I would just end up unemployed or maybe dead."

Devin sneered. "Now I know you've lost it."

"No, he's right," Nika said. "They might try to silence him. When my grandfather was young, he worked for a very bad man in Russia who operated with secrets and forbidden information. That man would do absolutely anything to keep those secrets from finding their way to the wrong people. If Harold is telling the truth, these types of people won't put up with someone who shares their secret. They would find a way to shut him up forever."

"Exactly," Harold said, puffing out his cheeks. "And Howard Dimwalls is that type of guy."

"Can't you just unplug it or plant a virus?" Cameron asked.

"I did plant a virus," Harold said. "But it's not that simple. This thing is designed to eliminate threats. Any normal virus I write will be sought out and destroyed almost immediately. But that all changes with you four in the equation." Harold crossed the room and knelt on the ground, his stomach pressing against Trevor's knees. "Your minds and abilities, if combined with the right virus, could access the central mainframe and destroy the data."

"But we're not computer hackers!" Cameron exploded, leaping up from his seat. "My intellect is sufficient to try, but the others are hardly capable. Even with years of study, we would never be equipped to gain access to the Adventure Machine's central mainframe!"

Harold blinked and a queer expression formed on his lips. "You don't get it, do you? You're already on the inside. You're already connected with the central mainframe. All I need you to do is initiate the virus."

Trevor paused, waiting for the punchline. "Do we just push some button?"

Harold grinned and then laughed. "That's exactly it! Just push the button. The same one you all started to push earlier." He once more glanced apprehensively at his wristwatch and gasped. "Oh no! We've gone way past the amount of time my hacking was supposed to buy us."

"There you go again," Cameron said. "*Hacking.* You said it earlier. You also used the word *glitch.* I may be brilliant, but you're not making sense, even to me."

"Look, I gotta go." Harold grunted as he grabbed Trevor's armrest and pulled himself up. One moved aside, and Harold pulled the door open. He wiggled sideways through the exit, sucking in his breath to squeeze out, and then he was gone.

"Are the Castletons really creating a weapon?" Devin asked.

"I don't know," Trevor said. "But it kind of made sense."

Cameron gasped. "It did? You understood that incessant babbling?"

Trevor smiled. "Well, not all of it, but I do think it's strange how the four of us were chosen to ride the Adventure Machine. It's not by accident. You know that."

"Yes, fine, I was the one who initially suggested that theory, but how are we supposed to put a stop to it?" Cameron stared at the floor. "Just push a button? Absurd!"

Nika slowly rose out of her chair, her arms wobbly as she

steadied her balance with the armrests. She stretched and flexed her fingers, staring down at them as if inspecting for fractures. "Whatever we decide to do, I feel I must remind you that I've been injured. I need to see a doctor and my grandfather immediately."

"I can help you with that," One said, his voice as smooth as a purring cat.

The monitor chirped on the desk, and the image of the intercepted email vanished from the screen. In its place a new live-action video feed appeared. Trevor noticed a man seated at a long table who looked strikingly similar to Doug Castleton, only he wasn't moving, and it didn't take more than a moment to realize why. Doug was bound to his seat by some sort of straps. Standing stoically like soldiers against the wall were the three remaining creatures, who appeared to be holding Doug as their prisoner.

"Why do they have him tied . . ." Nika caught herself before finishing, as the camera began slowly panning out. Several other adults sat next to Doug, also tied to their chairs.

"That's my mom!" Cameron leapt out of his seat.

"And my dad!" Devin gripped the sides of the monitor, squinting his eyes.

"*Dedushka?*" Nika's lips trembled as she noticed her grandfather in line with the others.

Trevor recognized the final prisoner as his own mom. He

whirled around, staring at One in disbelief. "What are they doing?"

One closed his glowing yellow eyes and sighed. "Our whole purpose of existence is one of survival."

"Yeah, we get that," Devin growled. "But what's that have to do with our parents? Tell your goons to let my dad go!"

One solemnly bowed his head. "I have no means of communication from this office."

"Fine. We'll do it, then." Trevor stood and started heading for the door, but One stepped in front of him.

"I'm sorry, Trevor, but I can't let you do that," One said, looking down at his hand and stroking a single clawed finger with his thumb. "We are designed to eliminate all threats. It is clear now to me that you four are our greatest threat."

"Gibberish!" Cameron shouted. "Everyone and everything at the Adventure Machine facility must speak gibberish. Nothing lines up. The past few hours have been a blurry mess of nonsense."

Trevor couldn't have said it better. How could One flip-flop so rapidly, when just moments before he had stood by Harold's side and helped them escape from Shrill?

One gestured to the chairs. "Please, be seated and calm your minds. It is easier for me to siphon what I need from you when you're at peace."

"Then let my grandfather go free," Nika demanded. "I will never be at peace as long as you're holding him hostage."

"Perhaps I should remove the distraction," One said. "Would it be better if I turned this off?" He moved toward the desk and reached for the monitor.

Trevor saw his chance and took it.

Lunging forward, he plowed his lowered shoulder into One's stomach and the creature instantly collapsed to his knees. One lashed out, slicing grooves in the back of Trevor's uniform and snagging the neotanium fabric with his claws. But Trevor's momentum carried him forward, and the force snapped One's hand back with a loud crack. The creature crumpled backward, and Trevor easily yanked open the door. He turned back to help the others, but they were already racing for the exit. Devin held the door for Nika and Cameron, then hopped out after, pulling the door to the secret room shut behind him.

CHAPTER 31

TREVOR DIDN'T KNOW how much time there was before something terrible happened to his mom, but he had to think of a way to save her and the others. The facility wasn't exactly small, and there were plenty of rooms throughout the building. And with the robotic voice continuing to squawk an "out of order" announcement from behind the closed elevator doors, there appeared to be no way off the main level.

Instead, the four of them followed the flickering lights embedded in the floor straight back to the Gallery. Racing up the tongue, they passed through the opening resembling a gigantic mouth, and from there Trevor pointed to the Terrorarium as a suitable hiding spot.

"We can't stay here long," Trevor said, leaning against the

side of one of the numerous video game consoles dotting the room. "One knows our next move too, remember?" He tapped his temple. "He's inside our heads."

The sound of cackling suddenly erupted from outside the Terrorarium. Trevor poked his head out from behind the arcade game just as Shrill Parker sauntered into view of the glass doors, coming from the direction of the food court. Her hair stood on end as if electrified, and she sliced the air with her meat cleaver. Trevor watched Shrill walk past, then disappear to the other side, her voice continuing to fill the air with her deafening laughter.

Trevor faced the others. "She's headed toward the lobby."

"Why is this happening to us?" Nika asked, almost on the verge of tears. "It was supposed to be just a thrilling adventure, one we would all enjoy. And now the absolute worst has happened. I'm seriously injured, and I don't want to think what will happen to my grandfather."

Trevor glanced over at Nika as another round of Shrill's laughter arose from outside the Terrorarium. But he wasn't thinking about Shrill, or One, for that matter. His brain raced as he tried to fit together the pieces of a new puzzle.

Cameron was still covering his ears with his hands, trying to drown out the sound of Shrill's voice. "This is my worst nightmare come true."

And then it finally clicked in Trevor's mind, the reality hitting him square in the chest like a medicine ball. The peculiar chain of events leading up to that moment, punctuated by Harold's words: *You're already on the inside. You're already connected with the central mainframe.*

"Oh man. This is crazy!" Trevor fell back into the console, his jaw dropping. "I think I've figured it out."

Nika looked hopeful. "Figured out how to get to my grandfather?"

Trevor shook his head. "I don't think we need to."

"Of course we need to." Cameron dropped one of his hands from his ears for long enough to scratch his nose. "I need my mom and my pills and two cans of Kraken Spit."

"No, you don't." Trevor got to his feet, a series of ideas swarming his brain like a whirlwind of gnats.

"What's wrong with you?" Devin stuck out his chin, his lips puckered to one side. "Why are you acting like a spaz?"

A knowing smile had worked its way across Trevor's mouth as he looked down, his eyes passing between them. "Don't you get it?" he asked. "Don't you see what's really going on here?"

"No!" the three of them answered.

"We don't need to save our parents because"—Trevor took a deep breath—"we're still on the ride!"

CHAPTER 32

"THE ADVENTURE MACHINE did exactly what it was supposed to do, and we all played along not knowing that the adventure never stopped." Trevor's eyes gleamed. "The Ganglion malfunctioning. The monster attack. Shrill turning into a real psychopath. It's all just part of the show."

Devin rubbed the corner of his eye. "That's the stupidest thing I've ever heard. The Adventure Machine broke down. There was smoke, and Cameron had to yank out a bunch of wires."

"Yes, what you're suggesting is simply impossible," Cameron added. "There are too many unexplained variables."

"Remember what you said right after the meteor shower?" Trevor asked. "You told us that they were projecting that

248

whole jungle scene with high-tech equipment and they used some kind of factory or factor . . ."

"Olfactory emissions," Cameron offered.

"Yeah, whatever. Couldn't this"—Trevor waved his hand around his head—"all be just a projection?"

Devin rolled his eyes. "You're crazy. That's just not . . ." He stopped when he noticed Cameron thoughtfully tapping his upper lip with his fingernail.

"I'm right, aren't I?" Trevor asked.

Cameron nodded halfheartedly. "You're right in the sense that the Adventure Machine could feasibly fabricate an environment such as our current surroundings."

"I knew it!"

"But"—Cameron held up a finger—"that doesn't explain all the other elements. The physical ones. Terry Castleton, for starters. He certainly wasn't some random projection."

"Why not?" Trevor laughed at Cameron's baffled expression. "All I'm saying is, how do we know Terry was actually there?"

"He touched me," Nika said. "He examined me for injuries. I could feel him."

Cameron sighed. "I'm sorry, Trevor, but there are more holes in your theory than an eroding asteroid."

Trevor licked his lips and thought for a moment. "What happened when that giant moose sniffed you?"

Cameron recoiled in disgust and looked away. "I'd rather not talk about it."

"It knocked you back, right? You could feel it."

"Yes, obviously."

"So was it a robot, then? It couldn't have been a real moose. They don't grow that big." Trevor folded his arms and reclined against the back of the video game console, everything starting to make perfect sense to him now. "You thought it was just a projection and it surprised you when you were proven wrong."

"What are you getting at?" Devin asked.

Trevor tugged on the neotanium material at his chest, flicked it with his fingers, and waggled his eyebrows.

Cameron frowned at first, but then his mouth dropped open at an odd angle. "The suit," he whispered. He stared down at his own uniform, running his hand down his sleeve. "It simulates feeling?"

Trevor nodded.

Cameron's eyes widened. "Of course! Why didn't I think of that?"

"Ha!" Trevor cheered, clapping. "I can't believe I figured this out before you. Look who's the genius now!"

"I'm not sure I understand." Nika's eyes flitted between Trevor and Cameron. "Are you saying that we can feel things that aren't actually there, because of what we're wearing?"

Trevor stood up. "When the moose knocked Cameron

back, he felt it through his helmet. When you fell into the hole, Nika, the impact was absorbed by your suit. This neo-tanium isn't just some way to protect us against the elements; it's what makes the elements feel real to us!"

Nika slumped on the ground, her hands pressed against her mouth. "But we saw our parents tied up."

"We believed we saw our parents, but in truth, they're not even there," Trevor said. "It's all part of the adventure."

"What if you're wrong?" Devin asked. "What if our parents are truly in jeopardy?"

"I'm not wrong," Trevor said.

"Then what Harold told us, and that lizard, was that all part of the adventure as well?" Nika asked.

Trevor hesitated before answering. Was that real or, like everything else that had happened the past few hours, was that all just a fabrication? He gnawed on his cheek and looked at Cameron.

"I think we were never meant to know those things," Cameron said. "Harold found a way to communicate with us through the Adventure Machine, no doubt violating numerous confidentiality clauses in the process, but it has to be the truth. Something sinister is happening within the walls of this facility. Something that, if not taken care of, could result in horrible consequences."

"It's up to us to put a stop to it," Trevor said.

Devin momentarily peeked above the video game unit,

before ducking back down. "So Shrill Parker isn't outside right now, planning a way to kill us."

The psychotic sound of Shrill's cackling drifted through the arcade. Cameron shuddered, his hands jerking up to cover his ears. Shrill sounded gleefully insane.

Devin held a finger to his ear. "You hear that, right? If she barged in here right now, swinging her cleaver, you'd just let her lop your head off?"

"Actually, that's exactly what I'm going to do." Trevor yanked sharply on the neotanium around his neck. The fabric resisted his pulling at first, but soon he felt it give under the pressure. The collar expanded, stretching wide, and a sizeable tear broke through, splitting his suit straight down the center. Trevor wrestled the rest of the way free from the clinging material, sighing with relief as he tossed it into a pile at his feet.

Devin cracked a smile. "Nice knowing you, dude. I'm guessing this junk isn't cheap, and you just destroyed it."

Trevor brushed his hands together. "Do I look worried? If Doug didn't want me to rip up his stuff, he shouldn't have lied to us."

Nika set her jaw in determination. "Will you help me remove mine?"

Cameron scrambled up off the floor, ripping at his collar as though his clothes were on fire. Trevor gaped at the small boy in amazement as he succeeded in removing the neotanium suit in record time.

Cameron breathed excitedly. "I can't tell you how desperately I've been wanting to do that since they first covered me in that hideous sheath!"

"Yeah, but just make sure you keep the rest of your clothes on," Trevor said.

Cameron looked down, regarding his turtleneck and jeans with disdain. "We'll just have to see about that."

Devin joined the others and removed his uniform, and the four of them stood facing the entrance to the Terrorarium. "All right," he said. "What's our next move?"

Just like everything else that had happened over the course of the past few minutes, the solution to their problem flickered on in Trevor's mind like a lightbulb buzzing to life. "We need to officially stop the ride, and I can think of only one way to do that."

Cameron gawked at Trevor in amazement. "How are you the one solving all the riddles? That's my job!"

"I guess I was born to ride the Adventure Machine."

"Don't keep us waiting," Nika said. "Tell us what to do."

Trevor grinned. "It's what we would've done in the first place, had we listened to Devin."

All they had to do was press their abort buttons, and those were lying on the floor of the Adventure Machine cart, deep within the Globe.

CHAPTER 33

CAMERON WATCHED AS Trevor casually strolled up to the entrance until the motion sensor detected his movement and the doors slid open. As Trevor started stepping through, Cameron hissed at him from behind.

"Don't just walk out there," Cameron whispered. "You've got to stick to the plan!"

"I was going to." Trevor leaned forward and peered around the corner.

"Well?" Cameron asked, looking hopeful once Trevor returned.

Trevor nodded. "She's there, right outside. Go take a look."

"Go take a look?" Cameron gasped. His shoulders drooped as he locked his fingers and breathed into his hands.

"If you're going to be able to do this, you're going to have to face your fears eventually," Trevor said.

"Easy for you to say." Trevor didn't have any fears to face. Cameron couldn't begin to count all of his.

Holding his breath, Cameron crept up next to Trevor and poked his head out past the door. Shrill sat facing the Terrorarium, her legs swinging back and forth over the side of a credenza displaying a few vases of flowers. The noise from the opening doors should have alerted her, but for the moment, Shrill seemed preoccupied with the sharpened end of her meat cleaver, skinning the edges of her fingernails against its blade.

"She can't hurt us," Trevor said as soon as Cameron leapt back into the room. "Remember that."

"I understand that you feel this way, but I'm struggling with accepting this as our reality," Cameron said. "Our helmets are off, and I can still see her. Maybe without our suits, she can still hurt us." How could Cameron, a *Whiz Kid Weekly* all-star, resort to following someone as impulsive and irrational as Trevor? There was no logic in it. And yet, Cameron could not think of any other option.

"All we have to do is make it to the stairs, down a few flights, and we're back where we started," Trevor said reassuringly.

"You're forgetting about the hole I fell down," Nika said. "And the collapsed ceiling."

"Does anyone have a better plan?" Trevor looked at Cameron and waited for a response.

Cameron removed his glasses and wiped the smudges from the lenses. There had to be something hidden in his mind. An alternate plan. One that didn't require squaring off with a complete lunatic wielding a sharpened blade better suited for shaving burlap! He swallowed. His throat felt lumpy and sore. No doubt the result of already having screamed in dozens of instances on the Adventure Machine.

"Okay," Cameron said. "He's right. We can't stay here forever. She's going to realize there's no way out except this way and face off with us eventually."

"Yeah," Devin said, nodding. "Might as well get it over with."

"That's what I'm talking about!" Trevor approached the motion sensor, and the doors slid open once more. "Follow my lead. And if you see Shrill, don't panic. Just . . ."

"Hello, children," Shrill hissed. She stood beyond the opening, holding her meat cleaver at her side. Cameron whimpered, hiding behind Trevor.

"Back up!" Devin said. "We can take a different way."

Cameron tried retreating, but kept bumping into Nika, who seemed unable to move.

"Don't run," Trevor said. "She's not going to do anything."

Shrill smiled. "I'm not, am I? Why do you say that?"

"Because you're a figment of our imagination." Trevor folded his arms, engaging Shrill in a stare-down.

"I'm not so sure anymore," Cameron squeaked. "Perhaps we need to rethink this." Shrill seemed real enough. There was substance in her movements. The matted hair, clumped with red goop. The streaky makeup staining her collar from all her tears. If she was indeed a fake, she was the most re-alistic projection of all time. Cameron had watched all sorts of documentaries on CGI. The greatest special-effects artists in the world couldn't have created something as lifelike as Shrill. Maybe they could try to reason with her. Promise her some of their prize money. Cameron didn't think the only solution was to square off with her in a battle to the death!

Shrill looked at Trevor, and licked her lips. "You're the brave one, aren't you?" she asked. "The one born without fear. Tell me, Trevor, will your fearlessness be able to save you against my chopper?" She twirled the cleaver in her hand, the gleaming blade sparkling beneath the fluorescent glow of the overhead lights.

"Take your best shot," Trevor said.

Shrill snarled, tossed the cleaver into the air, caught it with her other hand, and then swung out at Trevor's throat. The blade whistled, Nika and Devin screamed, and Cameron yelped. He wanted to look away but couldn't. He just hoped Trevor had been right about his theory.

Trevor never closed his eyes as the cleaver passed harm-lessly through him like vapor. And then Shrill vanished.

"Told you!" Trevor shouted.

"Holy cow!" Devin leapt forward, scanning the hallway for signs of Shrill. "She's really not here anymore."

Nika looked at Cameron, and they both burst out laughing.

"Were you worried at all?" Nika asked Trevor.

"Worried? Kind of," Trevor said. "There was a moment right before she swung when I thought I might have made a mistake."

Cameron gulped. "But you didn't duck? You just stood there! What if you had been wrong?"

Trevor shrugged. "Well, I guess you guys still would've had a chance to escape while Shrill was busy chopping up—"

"Stop!" Nika chimed in. "Let's not talk about it."

Cameron felt faint. Clearly, he had no clue about the inner workings of someone with a mind as complicated as Trevor's. Logic didn't play a role in his decision making. He was careless and wild. And dangerous. Cameron nodded em-phatically. And yet, without Trevor, where would they be? Would Cameron have eventually figured out the puzzle of the Adventure Machine? Would any of them? Cameron glanced up at Trevor, a strange sense of awe coming over him. They all needed each other. That much was certain. Whatever the reason they'd been brought together on the ride, Cameron wondered if anyone expected them to make it this far.

"Why are you staring at me like that?" Trevor asked, eyeing Cameron warily.

Cameron looked away. "I just thought of something," he said. "I've never had friends like you before." He glanced up, straightening. "We are friends, correct?"

Trevor looked around at the others before nodding. "Yeah."

"Of course," Nika said, smiling. "Are you all right?"

"I'm just glad," Cameron said. "Even though this has been stressful. Even tragic at times. I'm glad we met on the Adventure Machine."

Devin brushed past Cameron and peered in both directions. "It's not over yet," he said. "Why don't we save this for later?" He stepped into the hallway and motioned for them to follow.

CHAPTER 34

THEY DESCENDED THE three flights to the Globe entrance, their echoing footsteps providing the only sounds in the stairwell. When they reached the hole in the hallway, Trevor took a moment to test the wire's strength and found that, despite having dropped a few feet from its original position, it still held his weight. He swung across easily enough and passed the wire down the line. This time, Nika chose to go next.

Holding her breath, she pushed off from the edge, but unlike before, Trevor plucked her from the wire before she had a chance to fall and pulled her into his arms.

"Nicely done," Trevor said, steadying her with his hands. "What did you think?"

Nika smiled. "It was better than the first time."

"When we get off this ride, we should all go BASE jumping," Trevor said.

Nika blinked. "BASE jumping?"

"Yeah, it's where you jump off something really high with a parachute or a bungee cord, or something like that. Doug Castleton does it all the time on his videos. I bet he knows some pretty awesome spots in the area. Maybe he could even film us." Trevor looked back at Devin. "That would be cool for your YouTube channel, huh?"

Devin shrugged. "Yeah, sure. Want to give me some room so I can swing over?"

Trevor moved out of the way, and Devin whooshed across the gap. He wobbled uneasily once on the other side, reaching out and snagging Trevor's shirtsleeve to gain his balance.

"What do you think would really happen if I slipped?" Devin glanced over at Cameron, who was waiting patiently for the wire. "I mean, if it's all programmed by the Globe, would I really fall?"

Cameron exhaled dejectedly. "It pains me to say this, but I honestly don't know. We're all just following Trevor blindly. Maybe it would be better if we didn't explore the what-ifs and the unknowns at this time."

"Yes," Nika agreed. "We wouldn't want to give Trevor any ideas either, now would we?"

Trevor whistled as he leaned over the side, trying to see

to the bottom of the massive hole. "That's a long way down. It would be like BASE jumping, but without any way to stop."

Cameron made it across the hole next, and then, together, the four of them scaled the rubble mountain from the ceiling collapse and wound their way back to the room where the creatures had abducted Terry Castleton.

Nothing in the room had changed. It looked the same as when they'd left it: spilled paint cans, dangling wires, and the aluminum scaffolding they had moved aside from the door when they first entered the back hallway.

Trevor stepped over a pile of garbage and approached the door leading out to the track. He opened it, and the reddish glow of the maintenance light poured in from overhead. Trevor glanced over his shoulder and noticed the others eyeing the opening apprehensively.

"What's wrong?" Trevor asked.

Devin swallowed. "Is it just me, or does this seem way too easy?"

Nika nodded. "I agree. It feels like we're forgetting about something."

"Like what?" Trevor stared out into the Globe. Fifty feet away, the Adventure Machine cart lay in a heap, a few wispy tendrils of smoke seeping from the cracked hood.

"I don't know," Nika said. "But I think we should be cautious and stick together."

"Sure." Trevor grinned at Devin. "Bet you I can get there

first." He turned and sprinted up to the wreckage. Bending over the battered side of the cart, Trevor found his remote exactly where he had left it. If Nika hadn't been so concerned about her injuries, Trevor might have considered hanging out on the ride a while longer. Now that he knew the secret, there was nothing he couldn't do. They could be like superheroes, facing off against every monster and weird scenario thrown at them. But Trevor was tired, and eager to see his mom and tell her everything that had happened.

"Come on, guys," Trevor said when he noticed that no one else had joined him yet. "We just need to press these bad boys and then we're done." When he turned back, holding the remote in his hands, he discovered the reason for their delay.

"Trevor." Nika's voice trembled. "They're not fake!" The creature, One, stood beside her, his long black claws closed around her throat. Two of One's companions had their hands on Devin and Cameron as well. Even from the short distance away, Trevor could see the monsters were real. But how was it possible? They were no longer wearing their neotanium suits, which meant the creatures shouldn't have had any power over them. Unless they were something else. Machines, or maybe they were actors dressed up in costumes. But that didn't feel right either.

"The four of you will now return with me," One said, his yellow eyes twitching with agitation. "There is no need to resort to violence, unless you resist. And that's not going to happen, is it?" He moved his mouth within inches of Nika's hair, and he flexed his fingers before closing them once more around her neck.

"What's your problem?" Trevor asked. "Why do you keep messing with us?"

"I've learned much from you," One said. "But the others need their time to interact and grow. I promise that once we've gleaned all that we can, we will let you go."

"Like we can really trust you," Devin said.

One glanced back at Devin. "I have no need to lie. In fact, it's not even an option in my original programming."

"But you've evolved, haven't you?" Cameron asked. "If you've taken everything from us, then you'll have the ability to lie as well."

One chuckled. "I guess you'll have to make a decision." He turned back to face Trevor. "Either you come with me and we finish what we started, or you take your chances on your own and I dispose of your friends."

"I guess you'll do what you have to do," Trevor said, his thumb hovering over the remote button.

"If that's what you wish." One's eyes cut toward Nika. "She will be the first to suffer."

Trevor wanted to tell him to go ahead. That he knew for a fact this was all part of the show and that One had no intention of actually harming Nika. Trevor looked down at the remote. Maybe all that was left to do was push his button and the ride would stop. The lights would come on, and the creatures would power down like battery-operated toys running low on juice. It shouldn't have been such a hard decision. But what if Trevor was wrong and the plan backfired? He had already made quite a few mistakes. Almost everything that had gone badly throughout the ride could be blamed on him. He had put the others in harm's way, and he couldn't afford to make a mistake on this decision when the consequences meant life or death for his new friends.

A weird feeling came over him. It began in his chest, like the warnings of a cold. An achy, uncomfortable throbbing that made it hard to breathe at first. But then the feeling turned into a heaviness, which settled in Trevor's stomach. He had never experienced this before.

"You'll just free us, after it's all done?" Trevor asked.

"I have no need for four children," One said. "You'll just get in the way."

"What about our parents?" Devin asked.

"They're not of any value and will have the same opportunity to leave as you." One made a motion with his free hand, the one not currently squeezing Nika's throat, but he didn't move it far. In fact, the creature held his arm close to his stomach, protecting it as though he couldn't use it properly. It looked misshapen, maybe even broken.

"Come now, Trevor. Your friends don't know whether to

trust you anymore," One said. "It would be a shame for them to find out that they can't."

Nika, Cameron, and Devin looked exhausted, but Trevor also noticed worry on their faces and that made him want to throw up. He lowered the remote at his side and almost dropped it. But then his eyes returned once more to One's injured arm as he remembered something. Right after Trevor had rammed One in the stomach, the creature had dug his claws into Trevor's uniform. There had been a loud crack, like the breaking of a bone, and One had fallen away.

"What happened to your hand?" Trevor asked.

One cocked his head to the side and extended the forearm in question. "It is nothing."

Trevor scratched his chin. "Looks broken. Does it hurt?"

One smiled. "No, it doesn't. Fascinating, isn't it?"

"That's right." Trevor nodded. "You took on my fearlessness, Devin's psychic ability, Cameron's intelligence, which means you would've had to absorb Nika's abilities as well. Basically, you're just the four of us combined."

This caused the creature to smile. "I did indeed take from Nika. I'm now the perfect weapon. Advanced artificial intelligence."

"But you would've had to take everything from her, right?" Trevor asked.

Nika's eyes suddenly widened, and Trevor could tell she was thinking the same thing he was.

"You make a lot of bad decisions," Trevor said to One. "You probably got that from me. And you are kind of cocky, which I'm guessing you stole from Devin."

"Hey!" Devin flinched, but the smile remained. "That was a low blow."

Trevor shrugged innocently.

"And you're annoying," Cameron added. "Courtesy of Cameron Kiffing, I presume."

"What are you implying?" One glanced back at Cameron.

"That you took everything from us," Trevor said. "The good and the bad."

One exhaled a deep, aggravated breath. "I've had enough of our conversation. Say goodbye to your friend."

But Nika reacted first.

Before One could squeeze her throat, she raised her fists in the air and slammed them down as hard as she could on the creature's arm. One's fingers fell away from her neck.

"Osteogenesis imperfecta," Nika said, glaring into the creature's eyes. "You'll learn how to get used to it. I have." Then she kicked One in the knee, and his leg buckled from the blow, bending at an odd angle as he collapsed to the ground.

Devin elbowed his captor in the ribs and twisted free from its grip. The creature holding Cameron seemed unsure of what to do, and that allowed Trevor enough time to cover the distance between them and knock it to the floor.

"Are you okay?" Trevor asked Nika. She stared down at

her arms, and he could see the worry in her eyes. She had struck One with all her strength, and a blow like that might have broken her bones.

"Let's just finish this," she said. "I'm done with this adventure."

"Me too." Devin patted Trevor on the back. "That was awesome, by the way!"

"Indeed. You have an uncanny ability to think brilliantly on the fly," Cameron said. "I would love to see your official IQ test scores. I have no doubt they're much higher than I originally gave you credit for."

"Uh, thanks," Trevor said.

One attempted to give chase, but he hobbled along on the ground, unable to feel pain and yet unable to move much. "Your parents will suffer," he hissed. "They're still my captives, and I will never let them go." He reached out, dragging his body forward with his crooked arms, persistent to the end, now resembling nothing more than a smashed cockroach trying to walk.

"My mom's not there." Trevor held up his remote as the others grabbed theirs from the cart. "She never was."

"We do it simultaneously," Nika instructed.

"That means at the same time," Cameron said, smiling at Trevor.

Then the four of them pressed their buttons together.

CHAPTER 35

A SPRAY OF fog blasted all around Nika. She batted her hands, trying to see through the cloud, while rapidly blinking her eyes, but it didn't let up. The sudden burst startled her, more so than anything else that had happened so far on the Adventure Machine. Not that it was scarier, but because it was unnerving. Nika had no idea where she was or how she had gotten there.

"What is this?" Nika heard Devin ask from close by. "What's going on?"

"We need to evacuate!" Cameron shouted. "The Globe must be on fire!"

Nika sniffed the air. "This doesn't smell like smoke." They

would've been coughing and wheezing, and the fog had more of a pleasant, clean smell, like fresh bubble bath.

"Where are we then?" Devin demanded.

Trevor tried to stand up from the seat he now found himself in, but bumped into something rigid and heavy. "Ouch!" He massaged the spot where the flat end of a nozzle had struck his chest. He reached out, trying to redirect the annoying spray from dousing him.

"Oh, let's not do that," someone said. "We wouldn't want you to damage the equipment. Give it a second, and the fog will shut down."

It took a moment for the haze to disperse, but when it finally did, Nika saw Doug Castleton standing a few feet in front of the row of seats.

"Welcome back," Doug said, a twinkle in his eye. "How was your trip?"

Nika knew she must have looked foolish to Doug, because her expression was one of complete confusion. "We're in the Activation Room." She recognized the long decompression tubes and the soft, spongy chairs.

Doug nodded. "That's correct." Terry Castleton stood behind his brother, adding a few notes to his tablet with his stylus.

Devin raised one corner of his mouth, his nose scrunching. "Are there two Activation Rooms?"

"Just the one. It would appear that you're confused by

this?" Doug was recording their conversation with a tiny handheld device. "Do you have the data?" he asked Terry.

Terry held up a flash drive in his fingers and nodded. "All of it has been collected and is ready to be analyzed." Both Castleton brothers seemed tense, anxious. "Yes, Cameron, do you have a comment?"

Cameron once again had his hand politely raised. "I was sitting in this exact chair hours ago. I remember because when I sat down I thought it felt oddly like a marshmallow." He bounced lightly in his chair.

"Did you say hours ago?" Doug sidled over next to his brother, a shifty smile creeping across his mouth. "How many hours?"

"At least three," Nika said. "Though we didn't have a way of telling time."

"More like five or six," Devin added. "We were stuck on the track for a while."

"How did we get back here?" Trevor asked. "Where's the Adventure Machine?"

Doug winked. "You just got off it."

"No, I mean the cart that we rode in." Trevor pointed at the door.

Doug tugged on the handle, but the door didn't open. "That's not actually a door. It's just a decoration. Part of the whole ambiance of the ride."

"But Candy was in there," Devin said.

"Candy, like everything else you saw, is actually part of the program," Doug explained. "We're still considering other possibilities for that. Did you like Candy? Did she make you feel welcome, or would you rather it be someone else? We have a myriad of choices. How about a seven-foot man from Papua New Guinea?"

Nika reached up to rub her eyes, but stopped short of the visor. "Where did this come from?" She had taken off her helmet along with her uniform. When had they replaced her helmet?

"Are you all right, *Printsessa*?" Nika's grandfather asked from the entryway. "You seem distraught."

"*Dedushka!*" Nika sprang from her seat and raced for the door. But before she had a chance to fling her arms around him, her grandfather held up his hands to stop her.

"You know better than to run like that." Nika's grandfather leaned forward and lowered his voice. "You could've injured yourself."

"I'm sorry." She dropped her arms at her sides. "I was so worried about you, and now I know you're safe."

"Of course I'm safe." Her grandfather gently laid his hands on her shoulders and tilted his head to one side, studying her closely.

Nika jerked toward Doug, a feeling of dread swarming in her chest. "Is there a doctor here at the facility?" She looked down at her arms and legs, knowing there had to be numerous fractures. Even if the neotanium had somehow managed to shield her from her fall, she had fought One without any form of protection.

"We have a medical team on-site," Doug said.

"Why, Nika?" her grandfather demanded, his eyes widening with alarm.

Nika bowed her head, fighting back tears and trying to think of a way to tell him. She didn't want to admit that she had been wrong to ride the Adventure Machine. "I fell, *Dedushka*."

"When? Where?" He dropped to one knee, lightly cradling her wrists in his hands.

"In a hole. We had to escape these monsters and I swung across, but the wire broke free and I hit so hard. I may have broken something."

Mr. Pushkin stood and spun around, searching the floor. "What hole?"

"Not here," she explained. "It happened while we were in the Globe."

Her grandfather's eyes narrowed. "Is this some kind of joke?"

It wasn't a joke, but it felt wrong. How did they make it back to the Activation Room so quickly? Was there some sort of secret passage that they didn't know about?

Devin's dad entered the room. He snapped his fingers to get Devin's attention. "Hey, Son, why haven't you been filming this?"

"What?" Devin stared down at his lap. In his hands, he held his father's phone. "Hey, here it is!" He held up the phone, showing it to Trevor. "Oh man, I thought I lost it."

"From just walking into this room?" Devin's dad asked. "Maybe I should hold on to it. You'll end up breaking it."

"Excuse me, but when exactly are they going to get on the ride?" Cameron's mom asked, poking her head from behind Devin's dad. "It seems this sort of delay won't be good for customers, if you ask my opinion."

"Mom, my pills!" Cameron jumped from his seat and nearly tripped. "Hurry, before I have another episode."

"You just had your pill, dear," his mom said. "You don't get one for another two hours."

The expression on Cameron's face described exactly how Nika felt.

"Do you want to tell everyone here why our kids are acting like babbling idiots?" Trevor's mom asked as she stepped inside the room. "Or do we have to sign another contract to figure it out?"

Doug tapped his lips with his recorder. "Perhaps it would be best if we allowed the ride participants to fill us in." He held out his hands to the group. "Who would like to go first?"

"But you know what happened," Devin said. "You were

recording everything from our helmets. Well, I guess up until we got out of the cart and met up with that weird lizard."

"Now, that's what I'm talking about," Doug said, patting Devin on the shoulder. "It sounds like you all experienced an awesome adventure. One that I'm dying to hear about. And one, for that matter, that lasted only two minutes and twenty-three seconds."

CHAPTER 36

CAMERON HAD NEVER been so confused. Doug wasn't making any sense. It had been hours since they'd first hopped aboard the Adventure Machine, but according to all the adults, they had only sat down in the Activation Room just a few minutes earlier.

After assisting the four children with removing their helmets, Doug insisted he would clear up the confusion once he heard every detail of their adventure. Cameron did most of the talking, but the other three spoke up from time to time to add the bits and pieces of what he missed, all while the adults stood in an awestruck silence. Cameron told them about the Ganglion leading them into the prehistoric jungle, and the meteor shower, and the creepy moose attack. He told them about being chased by the creatures inside the Globe, Terry's capture, and Nika's accidental plunge into the hole. Cameron grew overly excited when he recounted the part involving Shrill Parker and her deadly chopper.

"Wonderful!" Doug said, clasping his hands together. "I really wanted you guys to experience the whole gamut, and it appears that you have."

"I think we need an explanation," Trevor's mom said, her arms folded tightly at her chest. "They all seem to have a very vivid memory of what couldn't possibly have happened."

"It did happen, Mom," Trevor said. "We didn't make it up."

"I never said you did." She smiled at Trevor. "Because how could you make up something so elaborate when you never left our sight? You didn't have time to discuss the details of this adventure of yours with each other."

"Did you drug our parents or something?" Devin asked Doug.

"Either drugged us or drugged you," Devin's dad replied, his nose twitching. "That's the only explanation, and frankly, I didn't give my consent for you to medicate my son."

Cameron jabbed his fingertips beneath his glasses and pulled down his lower eyelids. He needed something to soothe the impending headache, but according to his mom, he wasn't due for any sort of medication for another couple of hours. "Mr. Castleton, this is hurting my head. Did any of what we just told you actually happen?"

Doug leaned his shoulder against the wall. "My answer to that is both a yes and a no."

"Awesome," Devin grumbled. "I was hoping it would be an easy answer."

Doug cleared his throat. "Allow me to explain. Yes, you did experience an adventure in the realest form. But no, you never actually left your seat. You saw, heard felt, tasted, smelled, and endured a four-plus-hour excursion, which, in reality, took only a couple of minutes to complete."

Trevor turned to his mom. "Mom, we were on the ride for twenty minutes when it broke down. And then we spent hours trying to get back here."

"Are you trying to tell us that the whole ride was virtual reality?" Cameron reclined in his seat, his hands fitted behind his head. He had assumed virtual reality would play a role in their adventure, but only a minor role. As far as Cameron knew, there wasn't any manner of VR on the market that could simulate an entire experience without anyone being the wiser.

Terry slid his stylus behind his ear and replaced the cover on his tablet. "*Virtual* implies something created by a computer, and, while we did use technology to provide you with a virtual environment, your minds filled in the rest. Here, at our facility, we call what you just endured Cerebral Reality. Your senses feed your brain with information, and, in turn, your brain creates experience. What you saw, what you did, how you reacted and felt, all came from you. The Cerebral Apparatus connects the four minds by your consciousness, and then, of course, we added a few elements for direction. We supplied you with the map, outlined the schematic of the Globe and the Adventure Machine. We programmed the ride to stream your fears into a palpable atmosphere, one that would feel legit. And then, in order to truly create a terrifying scenario, we uploaded our creations into the mix."

Trevor pressed his palms into his forehead and then glanced up at Terry. "How did it go so fast? How did you make it seem like we were doing all those things and time was flying by, when none of it really was?"

"The Cerebral Apparatus is designed to tap into your mind. In a matter of a few seconds, your brain expanded and allowed the Apparatus full admittance," Terry explained. "The brain is the most complex and unexplored organ in the human body. There are facets and avenues that the most brilliant and recognized scientists have never even accessed. Through the Cerebral Apparatus, every particle, every cell of your brain is engaged, including your sensory functions. While virtual reality stimulates certain nerves and functions of the body, we engage them all in Cerebral Reality, allowing us to control time, distance, and perception. Seconds and minutes in real life could equate to hours and even days in the Adventure Machine world."

"Days?" Devin asked.

Doug nodded. "We haven't even begun to tap into the full potential of this technology. Imagine spending a week trapped inside the Globe, fighting for survival, being hunted by any manner of monster!"

"Sounds fun." Trevor's mom rolled her eyes. "So that's it? We're done here?"

"Not exactly," Doug said. "The contract states that there are some interviews we need to conduct, and we'll spend some time with the media later today. But don't worry about the particulars of that. I'll walk you through everything you should say on television."

"We're going to be on television?" Devin raised his eyebrows and glanced at his dad. Mr. Drobbs winked and gave his son a thumbs-up.

"Of course. There are at least a million and a half eager contest participants who want to know all about the maiden voyage of the Adventure Machine." Doug clicked off his tape recorder and slipped it into his pants pocket.

Cameron stood from his seat. "Contest?" Everything that had happened with Harold back on the ride came swooshing into his memory. The four of them weren't finished yet. They still had to put a stop to Doug's sinister plans. Cameron made eye contact with Trevor. He straightened, glancing fleetingly over at Doug and Terry before nodding back at him.

"So, when were you going to tell us the truth about this contest?" Trevor asked.

Doug adjusted the knot of his tie under his collar and smiled innocently. "What about the contest?"

"Oh, that it was just like everything else that's happened to us today. It wasn't real either."

Cameron sucked in a breath and waited for the worst to happen. He wanted it all to be fake. Finding out that the Castletons were evil and conniving didn't sit well with his stomach.

Doug looked confused at Trevor's statement. "I'm not sure I follow."

"You needed us," Nika said, moving away from her grandfather to stand by Trevor.

"*Printsessa,* what are you doing?" her grandfather asked, but Nika ignored him.

"That's why we won," she said. "We were handpicked to be a part of the Adventure Machine."

"Still stuck on the ride, are we?" Terry Castleton glanced awkwardly at the other adults in the room. "I think you're just hungry or light-headed . . ."

"Are you saying the contest was for real, then?" Devin asked. "Because I think the four of us can prove you wrong."

Mr. Drobbs nudged Devin with his elbow. "What are you getting at, Dev? You entered it yourself. I saw the website, and they had a boatload of people who submitted. How's that not a real contest?"

"Because they made it up," Devin said. "To find a way to get us here. They needed my psychic abilities. And Cameron's the smartest kid in the world."

"You really think so?" Cameron had been saying that the whole time, but to hear Devin speak it made Cameron blush.

"Trevor was born without any fear, and Nika has something wrong where she can't feel pain and her bones break all the time." Devin winked at Nika.

"How dare you talk about my granddaughter like that!" Mr. Pushkin bellowed. "You have no right!"

"It's okay, *Dedushka,*" Nika said. "Devin's not trying to be rude. I told them about my conditions."

"Why?" her grandfather demanded.

"Because we are being lied to," she said. "The four of us are truly unique. It can't be a coincidence."

"Listen, I think there's been a big misunderstanding." Doug motioned to the door. "If we can just get you out of your suits and take you someplace comfortable, like my office, we could have a calmer, more relaxed conversation."

"Just answer the question," Trevor's mom said. "Was the contest real or not?"

Doug opened his mouth to respond, but then turned to his brother for help.

"It's not that simple," Terry said.

"Sounds simple enough to me," Cameron's mom piped up. "And since we're the ones who signed a contract allowing you to play with our children's minds, I think we have a right to know."

The door to the Activation Room opened, and Mr. Crones stepped in. "Are they done?" he asked, leaning against the door to prop it open.

Doug no longer appeared to be in control of the situation. He smiled awkwardly at Mr. Crones, and looked pleadingly at the others in the room. "Please keep these unusual comments to yourselves and don't trouble Mr. Crones with them, okay? He's an important member of the California Theme Park Approval Board, and he's a very busy man."

"What's the problem?" Mr. Crones asked.

"Everyone's a tad excited, which is to be expected," Doug said. "But they're done. And as you can see, they're enthused, albeit perhaps a bit confused."

"We're not confused," Trevor said. "We know exactly what's going on. Mom"—he turned to Ms. Isaacs—"Doug used the Adventure Machine to steal our abilities."

Doug held up his hands. "I did no such thing. Steal your abilities? That's absurd. Look, you got me. The contest was a phony. We needed a collection of special minds to complete this project and you four fit the bill perfectly."

"That's dishonest. I know a fraud when I see one!" Devin's dad shouted.

"Fraud? No, sir," Doug cleared his throat. "We're the real deal. We're revolutionizing the world of thrill-seeking, and you don't accomplish that without taking risks. So we rigged an event to draw you here. So what? You're being paid, aren't you? You had the adventure of a lifetime, didn't you? Would you have allowed your son or your granddaughter"—Doug's eyes darted between Nika's grandfather and Cameron's mom—"to come to Beyond if I had just approached you out of the blue? I don't think so. We needed the contest to break a barrier."

"Then why are you selling the Adventure Machine technology to that guy?" Devin jabbed his finger at Mr. Crones.

"To Mr. Crones?" Doug shook his head.

Mr. Crones smirked. "Yeah, to me?"

"That's not his name," Trevor said. "It's something else."

"Howard Dimwalls," Cameron said, joining Trevor and Nika in the center of the room. "His real name is Howard Dimwalls."

Mr. Crones's grin erased in an instant, and the color drained from his already-pallid complexion.

CHAPTER 37

"**WHAT** DID HE say?" Mr. Crones turned his head and glowered at Terry.

"And"—Devin held up a finger, continuing—"Mr. Dimwalls isn't a lawyer or representative of the California Roller Coaster Club, or whatever you called it. He's actually some rich criminal trying to buy the Adventure Machine technology in order to use it to steal ideas." Bam! If Devin had had a microphone, he would've dropped it. He looked over at Trevor, who gave him a thumbs-up.

No longer smiling, Doug turned his full attention to Mr. Crones, who stood awkwardly against the door, looking like he very much wanted to leave. "That's impressive, wouldn't you say, Terry?" Doug asked, keeping his eyes fixed upon the lawyer. "The fact that these kids, with hardly any interaction with Mr. Crones, managed to conjure up such unique details?"

Terry's Adam's apple bobbed above his shirt collar as he swallowed. "Indeed it is. But that's what the machine is programmed to do," he reasoned. "Create realistic, imaginary scenarios for the participants."

Doug's eyes had taken on an apprehensive look. "And yet I've heard of Howard Dimwalls before. In fact, oddly enough, someone with that exact name approached me via email six months ago with a less-than-savory proposal. I turned it down, of course."

Mr. Crones fidgeted with the doorknob, his nostrils flaring. "What's going on here?"

"This is just the residual effects of having endured an intense experience. Nothing more." Terry glared at Devin and the others. "Where on earth did you come up with a story like that?"

"Oh, we didn't come up with it," Devin explained. "Harold told us."

"Harold?" Terry nervously scratched the side of his nose with the tip of his stylus.

"You know, Harold. That guy!" Devin pointed across the room, keeping his eyes glued to Terry for a moment before looking out the doorway. Harold Dippetts stood with a paper-wrapped churro clasped in his hand, powdered sugar coating his chin. Even though Devin and Trevor had technically only seen Harold from behind, sitting in front of his computer the night before, the man looked identical to the Harold on the Adventure Machine. And that was really just some virtual image. It wasn't real. None of it. If Devin had had more time to think about it, his head probably would've exploded.

"Do you know what they're talking about, Harold?" Doug asked, motioning for Harold to join them in the Activation Room.

"I—uh—I just got here," Harold stammered.

"We really should proceed with the debriefing," Terry insisted. "There's time-sensitive data we have to collect from the test subjects. Their memories are in a fragile state, and Mr. Crones still needs to file his final approval."

"Agreed. But I know a bluff when I see one." Doug approached Mr. Crones and faced him at the door. "What did you say your first name was?"

"I didn't say," he replied, his thin lips drawing into a straight line.

Devin felt his dad's hands squeezing his shoulders. He stared at the others. Trevor and Nika exchanged uncertain glances, and Cameron slid in closer next to them. Harold remained in the doorway, half a bite of churro showing from his open mouth.

"My name is Robert." Mr. Crones shifted his weight to his other foot.

Doug pulled his phone from his pocket. "Robert Crones, eh? Well, Bob—you don't mind if I call you Bob, do you?—let's just make a quick call to the CTPAB to verify your credentials, shall we?"

Terry cleared his throat. "That won't be necessary. I have all of Robert's documents right here."

Doug tapped his screen and selected the number. "Yeah, well, this will just take a minute."

"No, Doug, enough!" Terry shouted.

Doug lowered his phone. "I'm just concerned that with all our extensive research in finding these kids and putting them through our ride, our security may have dipped a little. Isn't that right, Bob?"

Mr. Crones wiped his palm against the side of his grease-soaked hair and stepped away from the door. "Well, I know when a deal's gone bad." He smoothed the lapels of his suit coat, the diamond-studded bracelet sneaking out from beneath his sleeve. "It was a pleasure meeting you in person." He nodded at Doug and then gave a slanted gaze at Terry. "You'll be hearing from my lawyers soon enough, Mr. Castleton."

"Right on. Stop at the reception counter, and we'll validate your parking," Doug said. "Oh, and in case you didn't already gather this, you are hereby permanently banned from the Adventure Machine facility. If I so much as catch a glimpse of your sniveling face within a mile of my property, I'll see to it that you're arrested."

Silence engulfed the room. Everyone's eyes were glued to the top of Doug's blond man bun as he stood, arms folded at his chest, observing Mr. Crones, a.k.a. Mr. Dimwalls, as he vacated the premises.

"Doug, I assure you, I had no idea—" Terry started, but his brother stopped him.

"You received the same offer from him, didn't you?" Doug said, turning back to confront Terry. "What I just can't figure out is why you did it."

"There's nothing to figure out." Terry sniffed. "It's all just a big misunderstanding."

"You were going to sell my technology to someone like Howard Dimwalls?"

"Wrong," Terry muttered. "I was going to sell *my* technology."

"Oh snap!" Cameron yelped.

"Yes!" Devin shouted in unison. The truth had finally surfaced. Devin pumped his fist in celebration. It was like solving a puzzle, or winning one of the trickier video games he played from time to time. Of course, Devin rarely struggled, unless he played online, which made it slightly more difficult to try to anticipate his competitor's moves. "It's just like we said!" He nodded at Trevor and Nika. "We figured this thing out all by ourselves!"

"Quiet down, Dev," Devin's father said.

"Do you think it was easy for me to work for you?" Terry snarled. "While you parachuted out of pilotless helicopters and wrestled crocodiles, I slaved away at my computer for long, thankless hours, creating this masterpiece."

"What are you talking about?" Doug demanded. "We did this together, and I always gave you the credit."

"Yes, but all while spoiling my life's work." Terry closed his eyes and sighed.

And that's when the familiar tingling triggered in Devin's chest. With all the excitement brought on by the Adventure Machine, he hadn't felt that feeling for a little while. But now Devin knew something was about to happen. He made eye contact with Trevor, but Trevor just stood there dumbfounded. He held up his hands and scrunched his nose in confusion.

"We have to do something!" Devin mouthed, pointing at Terry's hand.

"And I watched my research wasted upon your childish dream," Terry continued.

Doug flinched. "Childish dream? Why didn't you say something to me before going behind my back to someone like that?"

"Go to my baby brother and grovel at his feet?" Terry asked. "No thank you. And for the record, just because you made your fortune leaping into volcanoes and doing whatever other foolhardy stunts you've pulled over the years, it doesn't give you the right to own this." He held up the thumb drive. The one that now contained the Adventure Machine technology.

Devin lunged for Terry's arm, grasping for the drive in his fingers.

"Are you out of your mind?" Devin's dad demanded, grabbing Devin by the shoulders and holding him back. "What are you doing?"

"He's going to take it!" Devin shouted, pointing wildly at the thumb drive.

Doug looked appalled, but was incapable of responding.

Terry sneered at Devin, and slipped the drive in his pocket. "Tell me, Devin, did you *anticipate* me doing that?" he asked. "Well, it doesn't take a psychic to state the obvious." Then Terry stormed out of the Activation Room. He paused briefly to scowl at Harold, who had managed to finally swallow his bite of churro, and then continued briskly down the hallway before disappearing around a corner.

"Why didn't you stop him?" Devin demanded, shrugging free from his father's grasp. "You just let him go. All of you!" He glared at Trevor.

"I didn't know what you were talking about," Trevor said.

Devin sighed in frustration. No one ever knew what he

was talking about. He had to lay things out perfectly clearly for them to understand. He turned back to Doug, his hands shaking in anger. "Now your brother's going to sell it to that Dimwalls creep anyway."

Doug shook his head. "No, it will be fine. I'll have to take some sort of legal action to restrain him."

"Uh, no legal action needed," Harold said, poking his head into the room. "If everything went according to plan, which I believe it did, Mr. Castleton . . . er, your brother, Terry, is holding nothing more than a drive filled with corrupted files." A tiny uneaten piece of churro dislodged from Harold's chin whiskers and dropped to the floor.

Doug examined Harold thoughtfully, a look of wonderment forming in his eyes. "And exactly how were you able to make all this happen?"

"Oh, I didn't do much," Harold said, averting his eyes. "I just uploaded a simple virus. Well, I guess it wasn't that simple. Had to hack my way into the mainframe and stick a few glitches in place to intercept the kids on their journey. But don't worry, I made sure to leave the technology intact. I just corrupted Terry's thumb drive."

"Clearly, we've underestimated your expertise," Doug said.

Harold reached up and scratched the back of his neck. "Ah shucks, those kids did all the heavy lifting. They're the ones to thank."

"Is that a fact?" Doug glanced over his shoulder at Devin and the others.

"Well, us and the lizard, of course," Cameron said.

"That's right. Igrot." Harold snorted, his large belly quivering as he attempted to contain his laughter. "Igrot the Slime."

CHAPTER 38

FOR TREVOR, WATCHING Terry Castleton storm out of the room was the most bizarre thing that had occurred all day. And that was saying something. "That was real, right?" Trevor asked. "This all really happened. Or do we need to push another abort button?"

"I'm afraid this wasn't a part of the ride, Trevor," Doug said. "Though I wish it were."

"So you didn't know about your brother's plans?" Nika asked.

Doug frowned. "Of course not. I just wanted to give the world an adventure unlike any other. I apologize to you all. It was never my intent to deceive you in any harmful way. If you knew we were using your minds to manipulate your experience, it wouldn't have felt as real. But I never guessed they were *stealing* your abilities from you."

Trevor studied his expression. Doug appeared to be sincere. He may have been wrong to lure the four of them and their families to be a part of the Adventure Machine launch without knowing his real intentions, but it wasn't the end of the world. They had experienced something spectacular, and they would be paid a hefty reward for their participation.

"Well, I for one am outraged!" Nika's grandfather erupted. "You tampered with my granddaughter's mind. You made her think she was injured and that her life was in danger. She could be damaged. She could be broken in ways we cannot fix. I demand you—"

"Grandfather," Nika said, cutting him off. "It's okay. I wasn't hurt."

"It is not okay!" he shouted. "I will see to it he pays for what he did to you. I will shut down this whole facility!"

"No!" Nika stomped her foot, the sudden reaction startling her grandfather. "You do not understand. I am grateful for what happened to me."

Mr. Pushkin looked appalled. "Grateful? Grateful for these men playing a trick on your mind?"

"No, grateful for letting me experience something for the first time since I can remember. For once, I did not have to worry about leaving my room. I did not have to be told to rest and to avoid the things that every other child my age gets to do. *Do not do this, Printsessa. Lie down, Printsessa.* Do not be touched or touch anything. I helped my friends"—she looked at Trevor—"and they helped me and depended on me. I ran, *Dedushka.* I jumped and climbed and fought a monster. All by myself." She tightened her jaw, breathing through her nostrils. "You will do nothing to Doug Castleton, because he has done everything for me."

Mr. Pushkin stood in silence for several moments, squeezing his hands together. "Please." He motioned to Nika's chair. "Sit down. Be still." When she didn't obey right away, he offered her a warm smile. "I will do nothing. I promise."

Cameron cleared his throat. "Me too. What she said."

"What do you mean by that?" Cameron's mom asked.

"I may not have brittle bone disease or be forced to live cautiously, but I don't do much, aside from learn. I was scared on the Adventure Machine. I thought I was going to die and that maybe everyone else was going to die too. But then I realized if I wanted to live, I needed to help. And"—he swallowed, his eyes flitting between Trevor, Devin, and Nika—"they listened to me. And I may have annoyed them at times—"

"May have? Definitely," Devin chimed in.

"But," Cameron continued, holding up a finger, "they let me help."

"He did more than help, Ms. Kiffing." Trevor smiled at

Cameron. "He saved our lives." Cameron's head snapped around to look at Trevor, and his eyes seemed to glisten in amazement. "It's true," Trevor continued. "If it wasn't for you, I'd be down at the bottom of the Globe. We're bonded, remember?"

Cameron rubbed his thumbs over the lenses of his glasses and cleared his throat. "Well, technically, we weren't ever really in any danger. . . ."

"Oh, my little boy!" his mom gushed as she flung her arms around his neck and buried his head in her chest. Cameron's cheeks flushed a deep shade of purple as he shrugged away his mom's embrace.

"What are you thinking about, Trevor?" Trevor's mom asked.

Hearing his friends discuss their feelings about the Adventure Machine made Trevor think about what had happened just before the ride had ended. The moment when he realized his mistake could have resulted in their deaths. The gurgling pit in his stomach had all but disappeared, replaced with a hunger for lunch, but he could still remember the uncomfortable ache.

"It wasn't what I expected at all," Trevor said. "I think I did feel fear. At least, at one point I did."

"How?" asked his mom, resting her hand on the back of his neck. "Are you sure it was fear?"

Trevor swallowed. "I never worried about what would happen to me. I guess I was just a little afraid of what might happen to them." He nodded at the others.

Trevor's mom ran her fingers through his hair. "I suppose that's the best kind of fear there is."

"How about you, son?" Devin's dad cleared his throat. "Did you have one of those moments in which you realized your destiny?"

Trevor noticed Mr. Drobbs had once again started filming the exchange, his phone right on top of Devin's face. At first, Devin looked uncomfortable. But then he smirked.

"Heck no!" Devin said. "I wasn't even scared."

Nika clenched her hands into fists. "Not scared? Are you saying you did not run or scream or cry?"

"When did I cry?"

"Um, I think you cried right after that creature kidnapped Terry," Trevor answered.

Devin blew a puff of air. "Okay, maybe I was a little bit scared." He held his thumb and forefinger an inch apart.

Devin's dad chuckled. "You can't be scared if you know what's coming, right? I only wish this whole Adventure Machine thingy wasn't just in your mind. I have zero footage of you showing off your psychic abilities out there on the ride. We'll have to figure out some way to fake it. You know? Photoshop or something for when we post this video."

Devin smiled, but it looked forced. "Yeah, I guess," he said.

"Devin?" Nika pursed her lips, glaring at Devin expectantly. "Say something." She looked at Trevor for support, but she didn't know if this was the best time to get involved in a family situation.

"He should say something, shouldn't he?" Nika asked.

Trevor nodded. "Yeah, probably."

"What are you kids talking about?" Mr. Drobbs asked, panning out his phone to film each of their faces.

"We just think—" Nika started to say.

"I'll handle it!" Devin snapped, silencing Nika. Mr. Drobbs lowered his phone and studied Devin inquisitively. "It's just that"—Devin sighed, turning to face his dad—"I don't want *everything* to be filmed."

Devin's dad squinted and stroked his goatee. "Everything has to be filmed, but then I'll edit out the stuff we don't need later. That's how this thing works, son."

"Yeah, well, I don't want people to know about me like this," Devin said.

"Oh, so you don't want any subscribers on your channel, huh? Is that what you're saying? Because honestly, no one cares about just some regular kid. It's your ability that makes you special."

"That's not true," Nika chimed in. "He doesn't have to

have an ability. Mine doesn't make me special. It has nothing to do with who I am."

Nika's grandfather pulled her back and whispered something in her ear. Nika's face flushed from embarrassment, and she bowed apologetically.

"I apologize," Nika muttered. "It's not my place to speak."

Mr. Drobbs started to laugh. "No need to apologize. In two and a half minutes, everyone suddenly thinks they know about me and my son."

"I should not have said anything," she said.

"But she's right, Dad." Devin stared at the ground, his expression distant and unreadable. Trevor wondered what was going on in his head. "I don't want you to film anymore. Not right now, at least."

Mr. Drobbs slid his phone into his pocket and rubbed the corner of his eye with his finger. "Fine. If you want to remove some of the footage, I won't object. But we'll discuss this later. In private." He stared at the faces in the room, challenging anyone to object with his eyes. The silence felt uncomfortable, but Trevor was grateful that for once, the awkwardness wasn't directed toward him.

Cameron's mom cleared her throat. "So, about this check . . ."

*   *   *

300

Trevor reclined in one of the comfortable, cushioned leather seats in Doug's office, a large plate littered with the remains of a T-bone steak balanced on his lap. Nika sat to his left, spooning the last drop of yet another milk shake into her eager mouth. Devin and Cameron had finished their lunches, and sat, looking content and relaxed. A few members of the legal team had escorted the children's guardians to a room somewhere downstairs in the offices to finalize their payment, and a train of limousines had gathered outside in front of the main entrance, waiting to whisk away Trevor and his friends to the airport.

"I'm sorry for not showing you a true adventure, one not muddied by my brother's poor choices," Doug said, slumping in his chair and staring at the ceiling. He held a miniature model of the Adventure Machine cart, which he rolled across the walnut desk. Since his brother's departure, Doug had acted distant and withdrawn, his mind no doubt caught up in disappointment.

Nika stuck her spoon in her cup and placed it on the desk. "I don't think you need to apologize. I feel it was a true adventure."

"Yeah," Devin added. "I mean, it had everything. Suspense, mystery, thrills . . ."

"And we solved it together," Trevor said. "It was by far the most amazing experience I've ever had."

Doug examined the model cart one final time and then laid it aside. "You guys are being really awesome about this. And I'm glad you feel you got your money's worth."

"Wouldn't that actually be *your* money's worth?" Devin corrected him, raising his eyebrows.

"There's one thing I'm still struggling with," Cameron said. "If not to steal our abilities, why did you actually need us in the first place? All we did was ride the Adventure Machine. How could that have helped?"

"We needed data, Cameron," Doug said. "We wanted to see if your minds would break it, or if the ride would hold up under the pressure. Plus, we needed a way to test out the creatures. They are what makes each adventure unique. You four helped mold them into something more. With that data, we are ready to change the world with the Adventure Machine."

Doug stood and glanced at the wall clock, noting the time. "Well, your parents should be finishing up with the checks and paperwork soon." He nodded at Trevor's plate. "Are you satisfied with your lunch?"

"Oh yeah." Trevor patted his stomach. "Fat and happy."

"I have one more question," Cameron said, drumming his fingers on the armrest.

Doug folded his arms and leaned against the back of his chair. "Fire away, little man."

"Why exactly did you build the Globe?"

Doug grinned awkwardly. "Well, I love thrills and chills and spills. But I also love not having limits. To me this was the best way to experience everything, without—"

"That's not what I meant," Cameron interrupted. "Why did you build the ginormous Globe? If the riders are doing nothing more than just sitting in chairs, you could've done that anywhere. In a closet. In a hallway. Isn't that just a big waste of money to build a dome the size of a mountain, if you're never going to use it?"

"Did we build it?" Doug asked. "Are you sure about that?"

"Are you saying it was already here when you built the facility?" Devin asked.

"No, what I'm saying is that there is no Globe." Doug stooped over his desktop computer for a moment and then turned his monitor to give everyone a better view. "This is the security feed from the outside cameras monitoring the property. Notice anything different?"

Trevor could see the large building of the Adventure Machine facility, complete with columns and windows and the expansive front lawn sweeping down to the main stretch of highway. But the image was missing one crucial piece.

"Where is it?" Trevor asked. "Where's the Globe?"

Miraculously, the towering architectural monstrosity had somehow vanished.

"Like everything else here at our facility, the Globe itself is an illusion," Doug said.

Trevor looked baffled. "But how did you do that?"

"With the same technology used to send you through the adventure of a lifetime." Doug winked at Trevor. "I won't even begin to bore you with all the legal mess we had to wade through in order to construct the Globe. And it's not even real. But we wanted a way to lure the masses here to Beyond, California."

Unbelievable, Trevor thought. Doug had come up with everything. Even Cameron looked impressed.

A polite knock sounded at the door.

"That's probably your guardians." Doug made his way around the desk. "Come in. It's unlocked."

The door slowly opened, creaking as it was pushed inward, and a strange man stepped through. He was old, easily in his seventies, with wrinkled skin and white hair. He wore a plaid suit coat and a brown bow tie, and held a clipboard containing a thick stack of papers at his side.

"I didn't see anyone at the desk, Doug," the man said. "Must all be on lunch. So I let myself up, since I knew the way."

"Hey, Carl, come on in," Doug said, summoning the man into the room. "Kids, this is Carl Stratton from the CTPAB. He's an old friend."

Carl waved two fingers at each of the kids. "Nieces? Nephews?" he asked.

"Actually, they're the ride participants," Doug explained.

"Oh my. So young. How exciting this must be for you. Are you frightened?" Mr. Stratton looked directly at Trevor.

"Terrified," Trevor said, faking a shiver. The others in the room giggled.

Doug placed his hand on Carl's back and gestured toward one of the empty leather seats in the office. "I'm sorry that no one greeted you downstairs, but frankly, I wasn't expecting you."

Mr. Stratton fumbled in his suit coat pocket and produced a pair of thin-rimmed spectacles. "I'm fairly certain we had an appointment today," he said, examining his clipboard. "Quite an important appointment, as far as the board is concerned. Though I must say, I was slightly confused by the time. Terry's instructions weren't very clear on the schedule."

"Ah, I see." Doug leaned over Carl's shoulder to confirm the information on his clipboard. "And how's the gallbladder?"

Carl looked confused. "My gallbladder? It's been gone for years. Why do you ask?"

Doug smiled. "No reason. So you came here today to witness the launch?"

Mr. Stratton nodded. "Yes, and there's mention of a buffet afterward as well. I love the Castleton buffets." He licked his lips and beamed at the children.

Trevor laughed. Terry had forgotten to postpone the

actual inspection from the approval board. Chalk that up as another mistake made by the disgruntled Castleton brother.

"Well, that's unfortunate. I'm afraid you're too late. We already ..." Doug paused, his head tilting to one side in thought. After checking the time on the clock, Doug raced to the desk and pressed his intercom call button.

"Camberlyn," he said into the phone.

"Yes, Mr. Castleton," a woman's voice on the opposite end responded.

"How close are we to finalizing the payment for our guests?"

"We're just finishing up now," she said.

Doug pursed his lips. "Do you think you could stall for, I don't know, let's say two to three minutes more?"

"Of course, Mr. Castleton," she replied. "I can have them go over a few more legalities before we release them."

Trevor was already standing. Nika peered between him and Doug as she wiped her mouth with a napkin.

"Is he being serious right now?" Devin asked, slowly rising from his seat. "Or is he joking?"

"Oh, I hope he's joking," Cameron groaned. "He definitely seems like the comedic type."

Doug rubbed his hands together and pointed at Mr. Stratton. "We're going to have to really hoof it downstairs if we're going to pull this off before anyone's the wiser. Are you up for it?"

Mr. Stratton made a crooked smile and fixed his bow tie. "These legs may be old, but I was a sprinter in college some fifty years ago." He marched in place, his ancient knees firing off a series of pops like a string of firecrackers. "But why the hurry?"

"What do you say, kids?" Doug asked, turning to the group and looking each of them in the eye. "Are you up for one final adventure?"

ACKNOWLEDGMENTS

I always have to thank my wife, Heidi, and my children, Jackson, Gavin, and Camberlyn. They give me a reason to tell stories in the first place. A special thanks to my agent, Shannon Hassan, for pressing me to write a better story and helping me achieve my dream. To Tyler Jolley for reading and critiquing the first pages. To my wonderful editor, Rebecca Weston, for diving in and rescuing this novel after wading through the mire of my initial drafts. You truly are the hero of this book! Of course, to the entire Delacorte Press team for creating a beautiful package to share with the world. And to my amazing illustrator, Elizabet Vukovic, and Katrina Damkoehler, my cover designer. You captured my vision of *The World's Greatest Adventure Machine* and perfected it! Lastly, to my readers. Thank you. May you continue to find joy between the covers of books.

ABOUT THE AUTHOR

FRANK L. COLE lives with his wife and three children out west. When not writing books, Frank enjoys going to the movies and traveling. *The World's Greatest Adventure Machine* is Frank's ninth published book and his second with Delacorte Press. His first was *The Afterlife Academy*.

Learn more about his writing at frankcolewrites.com, find Frank L. Cole on Facebook, or follow @franklcole on Twitter.